D1561955

The Adventures of Gorgeous Katy

A COLLECTION OF SHORT STORIES

LENNA MASTAGEE

All Characters appearing in this work are fictitious. Any resemblance
to real persons living or dead, is purely coincidental.

ISBN 978-1-66789-588-8 eBook 978-1-66789-589-5

GUNNESS UNIVERSITY

It's the spring semester at Archibald J. Gunness University.

A University named after the 1812 war "hero" whose claim to fame was selling Andrew Jackson his horse.

School is all a buzz with the start of the new semester.

Ann Tobin, the school's student coordinator and financial aid officer, grabs Katy Rachford as she was heading to discuss a class change.

"Katy!", Mrs. Tobin yells after her, "Fred informs me that your GI benefits will run out next month. We love our veterans and I know it's your second semester in the Forensic Psychology Grad School program. We will try to get you some grants or other types of scholarships but in the meantime, we can put you on a monthly payment plan."

Katy, a bit surprised asks, "I've used it up already?! Mrs. Tobin, I will need to schedule an appointment with you to discuss my options. But right now, I'm just trying to get out of Professor Enzo's class. I heard he was a corrupt cop involved in the Lufthansa heist."

Mrs. Tobin quickly interrupts, "Katy, all these rumors about Professor Enzo are greatly exaggerated. He was maybe 5 when that happened. I recommend you stick with that class. It's very in-depth and like nothing else you will experience here.

Katy reluctantly agrees and instead of making that class change, she heads off to Professor Enzo's class.

Katy enters the classroom while Professor Enzo is talking about how the class is the 'reality of crime!' He further states that it is not a touchy-feely class... none of that nature vs nurture crap!

Meanwhile, a student named Tommy rolls his eyes as he whispers to Katy, "I heard the only reason he is still here is because he has blackmail on the Dean".

"Hey Mr. talking head what's your name?!", Professor Enzo directs his glaze towards Tommy.

"Me sir?! My name is Tommy Getter!"

"Oh yes! Your dad called a few times about you! A solid FBI career! Thank him for his service to our country! But you! Shut up and pay attention! Hey you! What's your name?!"

A nervous looking girl replies, "Brenda Chaplin".

"What's the matter?"

"I have anxiety," Brenda whimpers.

"Well, you better get over it. This class ain't for the faint of heart. S#*! That will probably get me another trip to HR", the Professor mumbles and then says louder "but I really don't care!"

Professor Enzo's focus now zooms in on Katy who is taking notes like a champ.

"Scribble scrabble! Ease up on the notes! What's your claim to fame?"

"First off my name is Katy Rachford," Katy retorts. She then begins to tell how her friend from the service was beaten and raped. She wrote her congressman to try to get him to force the military to act. She, on her own, got the leads that the police used and was able, with her congressional letter and criminal leads, to make the military and police take action. People went to jail and her friend received the proper mental healthcare that she deserved.

A very impressed Professor Enzo tells Katy that she is now in charge of Brenda and Tommy! He goes on to give more details about what's to come: There will be family members of victims and lots of crime scene photos and group projects!

Katy, Tommy, and Brenda leave the class when Tommy suggests they go to the bar to talk. On their way to the bar, a news brief comes on the radio about a homeless man found dead behind Blake's auto body. Tommy quickly changes station. Now, it's a commercial for Manny Estero. Tommy groans, "along with wanting to sell everyone's home he wants to be everyone's friend."

Katy half laughs, "I used to date him. But he had way too many bedtime lady friends!"

"How did you meet?!" Tommy asks.

"We met at the golf course where I worked the drink cart for a charity golf outing".

When they arrive at the bar, a smooth-talking Tommy strikes up a conversation with the bartender, Isabelle.

"Izzy, you're looking good and getting buff! But I'm sorry about your roommate Lauren moving to Chicago."

An unimpressed Izzy tells Tommy, "Shut up!" before turning to Brenda and asking her for her name.

"Brenda, please take Tommy over to the dart board and throw darts at him!" Izzy quips. Tommy laughs this off and orders two beers before heading off with Brenda to play darts.

Izzy then looks at Katy, "a horse walks in a bar and the bartender says why the long face?!, So why the long face Miss Lovely?!"

"Oh…hello…sorry, I'm Katy."

Katy extends her hand to Izzy, "I recently broke up with my boyfriend".

"Men!! They are too low for the dogs to bite!", Izzy commiserates, and she shakes Katy's hand.

Katy continues, "Plus, my GI bill is ending and now I need to come up with a way to pay for school."

Izzy gives her a sincere look, "Hey, Katy you are beautiful with that blonde hair and those big green eyes! I know you will succeed at anything you put your mind to."

Katy feels another set of eyes upon her. She turns around to see two men walk in. The one guy looking at her is familiar…maybe from the golf course. The other guy is yelling at him…saying something about not being more involved, "You gotta get your act together I want to retire and become a councilman, Franklin! I can't have any unsolved crimes when I leave."

Katy approaches the two men and says "Hello" to the one that she recognizes.

"Detective, right? I think we met at the charity golf outing,"

"Of course, you did!", the ruder of two men exclaims, "Franklin, here, would rather golf than do police work!"

"Give it a rest, will you Toomey?" Sighs Detective Franklin.

Katy snickers, "what happened to that poor man behind the auto body shop?"

LT Toomey is quick to answer, "there is nothing to worry about it's probably not a crime."

"Ok, thank you," Katy replies as she heads back over to Izzy.

"Geez... those guys aren't the most dedicated bunch of crime fighters, are they?!"

Izzy laughs, "Katy, I like you! Here, take this."

Katy examines the business card, Izzy hands her.

"Rodgers' lumber? What is this for?"

"Just come to the yard tomorrow. I might have an interesting new job for you!"

"Uh, Ok. great! Thank you."

"I hope you're up for action and adventure! Bring workout Gym clothes!"

Katy, in a not too confident tone, says, "sure ok."

Katy pulls up to the lumberyard and is greeted with a huge smile from Izzy.

"I'm so glad you came."

The pair go inside a steel building that's in the center of the property. It's full of workout equipment, mats, and a ring.

"Izzy, do you teach kickboxing or something?!"

Izzy laughs and says "no!"

They go into a small office where Katy is introduced to Brett Rodgers, the owner of the lumber yard.

"So, you're Katy. Izzy speaks very highly of you. Please have a seat."

Katy sits where Brett gestures. Brett goes on to explain that besides the lumber business he owns a small pro wrestling group, "My grandfather was into sailboat regattas and his dad loved sponsoring race cars on the local circuit. But for me, it's wrestling. Isabelle told me that you need a job. I also hear you are a veteran. That's great, that means you are disciplined and a hard worker. You can work at the shop helping Izzy with the books, but I have another offer for you as well.

" Oh yeah?! What is that?!", Katy asks.

"Try training with Izzy and maybe Betty and see if you want to give wrestling a go! You can start out slowly. Only one match a week and make the same amount of money as working 5 days in a coffee shop."

A bit taken aback, Katy, politely responds, "I don't know, sir. I'm not a very physical person. I like to run and do a little kickboxing but that's about it."

At that moment, in walks Hannah Glamour- the bleached blonde former star of that giant wrestling organization. She was seen all over the world but had some problems and was lucky to land a spot with Brett.

Hannah lets out a hearty laugh upon setting eyes on Katy, "who is this Kewpie doll?! I hope you're not trying to be a wrestler. You wouldn't last a week."

Following Hannah is Betty Bass, a long-time ring veteran! "Honey don't listen to Hannah she is just jealous of your youth.

"Shut up, Betty!" Hannah chides, "Let's go workout a match."

Katy turns to Brett, "Thank you, so much. I will take you up on your offer!"

Izzy shouts, "that's my girl! I knew you were a tiger!"

For the next few weeks Katy balances school, bookkeeping and wrestling. Betty Bass has helped Izzy teach Katy the ropes and has agreed to be Katy's first opponent. They are brainstorming to try and come up with a ring name for Katy! They try Katy Crème brûlée Rachford?! Nope! Katy new romantic Rachford? Nope!

They are stumped.

Hannah walks over. "What are you losers doing?".

"Creating a ring name for Katy!" Betty says.

"I don't care what you call her. Just give me the chance and I will crush that gorgeous face of hers.

"Hannah, what did you say?", Brett asks "What did you call her?! Gorgeous?! That's it! Gorgeous Katy!"

A very upset Hannah storms off!

The day of Katy's first match has arrived!

"Just follow my lead and we will work through it together!" Betty tells a very nervous Katy, "If the crowd takes a liking to you then we will have you win in the end. The match is in front of a very small crowd."

Izzy gives Katy a hug, "this is it! Follow Betty and you will be great! Go get her!"

Katy, all decked out in her pink robe and matching pink suit, quietly makes her way to the ring. She hears the ring announcer declare, "You all know Betty Bass".

The crowd boos!

"But making her wrestling debut is Gorgeous Katy!"

The crowd is quiet, at first, but then they get a good look at Katy and start to cheer!

The bell sounds and Katy spins around Betty with ease. She gives Betty a boot to the butt sending her into the ropes! The crowd laughs and cheers! Katy runs and springs off the ropes leaping up to catch Betty in a high cross body block! Betty catches her and tosses her to the mat! Betty beats on Katy but Katy is hanging tough! The crowd admires her spunk! After several near fatal mistakes Katy catches Betty with a dropkick! Betty goes down like a redwood tree! Katy grabs Betty's ankles and does a front flip! Katy has Betty folded in half! The ref counts 1! 2!! and 3!! Katy springs to her feet and the crowd cheers!

"In her debut match! The winner is Gorgeous Katy!"

The crowd loves it.

Katy exits the ring.

Bobby and Becky Jasper, two twins and huge wrestling fans, ask Katy for her autograph! Katy is shocked but gladly signs! They tell her that they love her and want her at their wrestling themed birthday party!

"Absolutely kids!" Katy grins.

Katy is on cloud nine as she makes her way back to the dressing room..

"You did great!" Betty and Izzy say in unison as they sandwich her in a group hug!

They are so, so proud!

At her next reality of crime class Katy notices that Brenda is not there. She looks at Tommy and mouths "where is she?!"

Tommy gestures back with his hands "I don't know!"

"Today, we have a guest speaker, Ms. Tasha Williams."

The guest speaker shows two pictures: one of her son with a smile in his baseball uniform and the second of him in a coffin. She pleads with the class that none of his counselors or teachers did a thing. Her baby fell into the wrong crowd and was killed. She asks them if they go into psychology to please don't disregard the minority communities.

Tommy catches up with Katy after class.

"Wow that was deep!"

"So sad."

Mrs. Tobin catches up to the pair and pulls Katy aside. "Katy. Sorry but Fred keeps reminding me that your tuition bills are accumulating. "

"Yes, I know Mrs. Tobin, I will come see you."

Katy's phone rings and she excuses herself to answer, It's Izzy all in a panic!

Did Katy hear that correctly? Did Izzy say that "Brenda is dead".

"Izzy drink some water. We are on our way. Tommy, come on we must get to Izzy at the bar!"

A confused Tommy asks Katy, "what, why, what the hell happened?!"

"I'm not sure. Something terrible, I think. Let's go!"

They arrive at the bar and Izzy is all flustered.

"I found Brenda while taking out the recycling!" She starts upon seeing Katy and Tommy. "She was just sitting there lifeless against the dumpster!"

Detective Franklin and LT Toomey come in from outside and Katy hits them with 1000 questions. "How did she die?! Did she overdose? Can you check for video cameras?! Was she robbed or raped? Please tell me what happened?!"

Det. Franklin says there was no sign of rape, and she had her money and ID on her.

Katy then asks what she was doing behind the bar, but Franklin again has no answers. He tries to tell Katy it might just be a horrible accidental overdose or a suicide.

"We will have to wait for the tox report", he tells Katy.

Katy turns to LT Toomey, "Sir, if there is anything I can do please let me know."

The LT sternly looks at Katy, "Keep out of it. This isn't a game of cops and robbers. This is an ongoing investigation."

The police finish up with their photographs and the coroner takes Brenda away. Katy goes over and hugs Izzy and they let out a good cry.

Katy then stands up and stiffens her spine, "I don't think those guys care at all. Tommy, do you know where Brenda lives?!"

"Yeah, the Bonwit apts."

"Ok. I know the place." Kays answers, "that building is owned by Manny's father."

She then turns to Izzy, "come on you can stay with me tonight."

A couple days later after listening to an LA Police Officer talk about gang violence. Katy and Tommy tell Professor Enzo all about Brenda.

"I was informed," he says as he shakes his head, "….and from the looks of it, the police think it's either an overdose or a suicide." But he sees the pain in Katy's eyes. "Don't worry, Katy, I will speak to my old informant Eddie Galindo. I got him at welding job at the metal shop on 3rd. He owes me. Tommy, take Katy home and just relax. You too, Tommy. Relax. You've both been through a lot."

Katy and Tommy leave as ordered but Katy immediately tells Tommy to take her to see Eddie. "No way! You heard, Enzo, we should just go home and rest. He said it's most likely an overdose."

Katy grabs Tommy by his shirt collar and yells, "take me right now!"

With a sigh, Tommy says, "ok, ok but now you have to get me a date with Izzy!"

"Fine let's go!"

They arrive at the metal shop and see Eddie. They say they are friends of Ray Enzo.

He looks them up and down, "you're not cops."

"Obviously," says an annoyed Katy. "We're not here to bust your balls. We just want to know if you know anything about our friend who died and if you knew the homeless man who died too?"

"Oh yeah Charlie Brown, no Bruen, nice bum I gave scrap metal to sell. A damn shame I didn't know that he had any trouble with anyone. As for your friend what was her name?!"

"Brenda." Replies Katy.

"Oh yeah, the girl with the drug overdose. Well, I don't know anything about that, but I will ask my man T. He deals Xanax and Adderall to all the college kids. But it's gonna cost you a carton of Newport's and fifty bucks. I usually ask for a hundred but since you're friends with Ray I will do it for fifty."

In class the next day they learn about Petechial Hemorrhages! The Professor tells the class, "Have a good one; now scram."

But he makes sure to grab Tommy and Katy before they can exit the class.

"Hey, dopey Tommy and Nancy Drew, you two stay behind", he yells.

A very red-faced Ray Enzo screams, "don't you ever talk to Eddie again. You don't know him. He is not a good guy. We still don't know if anything is going on."

He looks over at the pair. That put a little scare into them. Okay, calmer this time.

"Let me tell you something, there are real monsters in the world. You don't want to get mixed up with them. Because no matter how hard you try a little monster rubs off on you! It changes you and not for the better. Plcase don't become one. Join the chess club. But I give you my word. Which I hate to do, but if anyone did anything to one of my kids, my students, I will personally get involved. Now beat it!"

Katy and Tommy get out of there as quickly as they can. As they leave they once again encounter Mrs. Tobin.

"What a great deal I worked out for you Katy. After some grants and a small scholarship from the school, you will only have to pay about 1400 a month. "

Fred runs up to Mrs. Tobin and corrects her, "no, it's 1500."

A disheartened Katy sarcastically says, "thanks a lot, Fred."

As they walk away, Katy looks over at Tommy, "Wow, that's a lot to pay along with my rent!"

"Move in with Izzy! It's a win-win! You get cheap rent and I get to drop by and romance Izzy. By the way Katy, you still owe me a date with her.

Katy giggles, "yes I know."

It's a great idea. So, Katy moves in with Izzy. She is in her room decorating when Izzy walks in.

"Wow the place looks great! Now we can both save money. Katy, come follow me into the TV room. I owe you something."

Katy follows. Izzy spins around, puts Katy in a headlock and gives Katy nuggies!

"That's for making me go out with Tommy!"

They stumble and fall on the couch, laughing.

"He ain't that bad, Izzy!

"You got me there, Katy. I've seen worse!"

"Alright I got to call Manny."

Katy makes her phone call. She tells a very happy Manny that she is coming to see him.

"I will make time for you, please swing by", Manny tells her.

Katy hangs up and tells Izzy, "I know it sounds crazy, but I have a sixth sense about murder. It's an old feeling I haven't felt in a while."

Izzy grabs Katy, "I got your back 100 percent! But I have a sixth sense about wrestling. Everyone thought you were gonna quit or fall flat on your face! You showed them all. You have something special. Not so much as a phenomenal athlete but you have a connection with the people. I've never seen a crowd take to someone so fast. So after we roll around and make a few bucks at that kids party we have that big tag team match! Katy if we win that match you will be a star!"

"Ok but only after justice for Brenda."

"Yes, we will get her that!"

The next day Katy arrives at Manny's office. He is in an Armani suit showering Katy with a big old grin. He gives Katy a big hug! Katy wasn't feeling it so much.

"Katy baby what can I do for you?!"

She asks about Brenda.

"So sad. A drug overdose I hear."

"How long was she living here?!"

"About a year or so."

"Did she pay her rent on time?!"

"No, her parents always paid."

"Did she have any problems with anyone??"

"No, no. She was a great tenant. Listen, baby, if I hear anything I will call you right away."

Katy leaves quite puzzled. What really happened to Brenda?

Now it's the afternoon of Bobby and Becky Jasper's wrestling party. The yard has the ring right in the center! The grill is cooking the cotton candy machine is churning. Izzy the lady warrior Salinas makes her way through the yard to the ring! The kids go crazy and climb all over Izzy! She picks up Becky and puts her on her shoulder carrying her all around the outside of the ring! But from inside the ring Sally Slick is standing there in her purple wet look one piece.

She yells at Izzy, "Drop that brat and get in the ring!"

The kids boo their brains out at Sally! Izzy hops in the ring and it's go time! They trade forearm smashes and tomahawk chops! Sally whips Izzy into the ropes! Izzy bounces off and nails Sally a flying knee to the midsection! Wow! Sally goes down! From there it's pitched battle going back and forth! Izzy finally has had enough! She hits Sally with elbow to the nose! Izzy picks up a stunned Sally and gives her a pile driver! Incredible! Izzy covers Sally for the 1! 2!!! 3!!! Izzy wins! The kids go nuts!

Betty takes Katy to the side of the house, "to be big you need to fall. This is not a league match so Katy let's see how you handle being on the losing end! Don't worry you will do great!"

Betty in her 1982 black and gold reinforced one piece waddles her way into the ring!

The kids all boo! Then Bobby and Becky's mom yell, "there she is kids it's Gorgeous Katy!" Katy stops and signs autographs and takes a few selfies! Boy the kids are in love with Katy! Katy jumps in the ring looking like a pink princess! She waves at the kids and Betty charges at her like a bull! Wow! Katy dashes away and Betty slams into the corner turnbuckle! She turns around and charges again! Katy grabs her wrist and swings Betty to the mat! The kids cheer! It's a close contest as Betty does her best to cheat and Katy tries to stay one step ahead of Betty! Next thing you know Betty goes down! She is hurt! Katy lets the ref check on her while she waves and talks with the kids! They all start yelling she is faking she is faking turn around!

"No, no I don't want to beat a hurt opponent! That's not fair!" Katy insists.

Then suddenly Katy gets a knee to the back! Ouch! Then she is spun around and gets a boot to the belly! Oh, my Betty picks up Katy and power bombs her into the mat! The kids all boo!! Betty flops on top of a dazed Katy and goes for the pin! The ref counts 1! 2!! and Katy gets her shoulder up Betty holds her down again and again Katy valiantly kicks out! Betty leaps up and drops her big butt right on Katy's chest! Oh no! That's it! The ref counts 1! 2!! Katy tries with all her might but can't kick out! The ref counts 3!!! Betty wins! The kids boo and shout Katy got robbed! Katy gets up slowly and tells the kids, "No, No! You can't win them all we will get her next time!"

The kids cheer and shout "Katy! Katy!"

Betty and Izzy meet Katy behind the house. "That was great!", they both tell her. They never knew anyone who lost and still got so much praise!

"Come on, Katy, let's go." Izzy says to Katy, "Enough of this kiddie stuff. Tomorrow it's the Doom sisters!"

Katy spends the next morning in bed searching the web trying to find any more info about Brenda and Charlie. She calls and leaves messages for both Detective Franklin and for her Ex Manny!

Izzy comes in her room and says, "any luck?"

Katy sighs, "no."

"Well, you're doing all you can. I'm proud of you. But now let's go hammer the Doom Sisters and make you a star!"

Katy cracks a smile, "You are one of a kind Izzy!"

Katy and Izzy arrive at the indoor soccer field. It's the largest crowd yet for Katy!

Izzy tells Katy, "This isn't a scripted match. The Doom Sisters want to hurt you and win!"

"As long as you're with me Izzy we got it made!" Katy jokes.

Debbie and Donna Doom are already in the ring. Betty tells Katy and Izzy to run right in the ring and unload on them, take them by surprise!

"I love you girls be careful!" Betty yells after them as they enter the ring.

Izzy and Katy walk slowly to the ring gingerly waving to the crowd when Izzy says "Go!"

They run full speed and slide right under the ropes into the ring! They take the Doom sisters completely by surprise! They have them on their heels reeling! The crowd loves it! Things settle down and the Doom Sisters do what they do best! They beat you down and cheat at every turn! Things are looking bleak for Katy and Izzy! Katy is out on the ring apron flat on her back! Izzy just barely kicks out of another pin attempt from Donna! Katy tries to get to her feet! She pulls herself up with the ropes! She yells at Izzy to tag her in! Katy got hurt early and Izzy was left alone to battle two giants.

Katy screams "tag me Izzy! "

With her last ounce of energy Izzy pushes Donna aside and makes the tag! Katy comes in like a screaming banshee! She knocks the wind right out of Donna with a double mule kick! Donna goes down and Katy hits her with a snap elbow and goes for the pin! But in comes Debbie she leaps up to crash down on Katy, but Katy rolls away! Debbie crushes Donna instead! Debbie gets up all confused and gets drop kicked right out of the ring! Katy covers Donna as the ref and the fans count 1! 2!! 3!!! They did it! They did it! Izzy and Katy win! The crowd goes berserk! Betty greets her two battle weary heroes with some great big hugs! Izzy and Katy just lean on each other completely exhausted!

Betty throws on Katy's robe and says, "look at me I'm Gorgeous Katy I'm so sweet! Sweet as sugar but with the heart of a lion! I'm so proud of you girls, let's go celebrate! Drinks are on me!"

Betty tells them to shower and get some clothes as she goes to get the car. Betty, happy as a clam, strolls to her car still wearing Katy's robe! When bam! She gets hit from behind! But, tough as nails Betty fights back sending the attacker running. Betty feels a tiny scratch on her arm? Was it a pin or needle or something?! Then things get blurry for Betty. She just manages to stagger back to the dressing room. She walks in and says "I was attacked" before collapsing on the floor. Izzy calls an ambulance while Katy holds Betty.

"Please, Betty, stay with me!" Katy pleads with her.

At the hospital Betty is in rough shape. The Dr comments that "she is one tough lady".

He continues, "we think it might have been a heart attack, but we are also taking blood samples due that cut on her arm in case someone tried to poison her."

Det. Franklin comes in and Katy goes off on him, "She was wearing my robe that should have been me!"

Det. Franklin tells her, "Calm down! All we have now is a possible pervert trying to cop a feel." "What about that cut?! What about her passing out so quick?!", Katy snaps.

"Maybe she had heart attack from the shock of the attack. But they are taking samples to test for any type of poison or drug. She is in good hands. Please go home and come back when she is stable," Det. Franklin tells her.

Katy is in class and her head is spinning! She doesn't give a damn about the Lindbergh kidnapping! As soon as class is finished Katy and Tommy rush Professor Enzo! She goes 90 miles an hour talking about how she was in this pro wrestling match, and they won and her friend was wearing a robe! She goes on to say her friend was attacked and almost died and since she was wearing Katy's robe is convinced that the person who attacked her friend was really after her!

"Slow down.", the Professor tells her, "First of all you did what?! You?!! A pro wrestler?! Umm ok! But you said your friend was attacked and it was supposed to be you?!

"Yes! Yes!" Katy says.

Now Professor Enzo is starting to get concerned.

"First take a few deep breaths then get something to eat! Do it! You need protein at a time like this. Then later you will go to the hospital and see if you can talk to your friend. I will try to find out anything that may have been caught on video. I will also personally put the screws to Eddic to try to find any link between Charlie the homeless guy and Brenda."

Obeying orders, Katy and Tommy get a bite to eat then go to the hospital. Betty is awake and in good spirits but not out of the woods yet.

"I can't remember much because the attacker had a mask and gloves." Betty tells her friends. "Blood tests have been inconclusive for any poison. Not a big enough dose if I got exposed to anything. I spoke to Brett, and we agreed that you, Katy, should face Raquel Ruthless in my place. Winner goes up against Hannah.

Katy looks down at Betty laying in the hospital bed, "now is not the time to talk about that. You could have been killed!"

"Honey, I've been in much bigger scrapes than that! It's quite alright! Plus, we don't even really know what happened."

In awe, Katy says, "I can't believe you can be so calm. Ok, ok, let's talk about it. But if anything, it should be Izzy!"

"Izzy is going to start up her feud with Scarlet O'Horror. It will be epic.", Betty says. "It's perfect you already have a win over me!"

"Yeah," Katy replies. "But you beat me at the Jasper party!"

"That wasn't a league match. Don't worry, you are ready!! "

Katy leans over Betty and gives her a big hug and kiss on the forehead! "You're crazy but I'm going to let you rest now."

Katy and Tommy leave.

Tommy looks at Katy, "I can't believe someone would want to hurt you, Katy. It is now my duty to take you home!"

They get to the apt and Tommy wastes no time to start flirting with Izzy, "my dear Isabelle your knight in shining armor is here!"

"Are you kidding me?! How can you protect us?!, Izzy laughs.

"I was a master of mortal combat!"

"What style of combat?! "Izzy scoffs.

"The video game!!" Tommy exclaims.

With that, Izzy laughs and throws him out the door!

Katy sits down and sighs what a day! No luck with Betty but Katy tells Izzy all about the match that Betty now wants Katy to have with Raquel. She then asks all about Izzy's feud with Scarlet.

"Girl we are going to train hard! We are gonna kick each other's butts to be ready!" Izzy tells Katy.

"I can't believe we are still talking about wrestling!" Katy responds looking quite upset.

Izzy, in her most cheerful tone, "Never ever let fear stop you from any-thing! Plus, my mom prays for our safety 5 times a day! So, we are in good hands!"

They have a beer toast to celebrate their upcoming victories and to thank Izzy's mom for being their guardian angel!

After a long and intense lecture on all the havoc The Son of Sam caused in NYC, Tommy and Katy stayed after class. Professor Enzo takes the opportunity to feel them in on what he has learned. Enzo isn't convinced that Charlie and Brenda's deaths are related in any way but he did do some asking around and even hit up some private eye friends of his. He tells Tommy and Katy that Charlie Bruen was a stockbroker who put all his money in with that Billionaire Fraudster Barry Mardove! So, in the 2008 crash he lost everything along with his wife and kid who left him. Not only that but he lost a huge sum of money belonging to the real estate brokerage of Mateo Estero.

Katy gasps, "that's Manny's dad!"

Enzo, surprised, "you know him?! And he knows you?! Well guess what?! Brenda Chaplin made numerous complaints to the building department about her apt. Unlicensed electric work! Rats in the basement and false elevator inspection sheets! They were hit with massive fines and almost had the whole apt complex condemned."

"Whoa this is getting a bit much for me!" Tommy pipes up. "I came to get my degree and scam the rest of my life. Not get caught up in a murder ring! Izzy is a smoke show, but I think Kelly Barrett from last semester might still like me!"

"Relax Mr. Hero Romeo! Don't run for the hills yet." Professor Enzo tells him. "We still don't know how they died. Hopefully if there is something strange in both their systems then the Police will have to act. Let's wait and see."

"What about Katy?! Who attacked her?! Or more correctly thought they were attacking her?" Tommy asks. He really is concerned.

The Professor tries to assure them. "Nothing in Betty's system, right? She had a little cut but that could have been from anything! Maybe it was a perv! That does bother me a bit, but it could be totally unrelated! For now, Katy try to always be with someone if you're going out at night. Just to be overly safe. Here's the deal! The information I have obtained, the police can get it as well. If not, we can make sure it ends up on the right desk. Let's stay positive until God forbid, we have to turn negative."

Katy and Tommy leave the classroom and run right into Fred!

"Ms. Rachford, we need your monthly funds, or I will be forced to inform the bursar's office."

"Turn around, Fred."

Confused, Fred follows Katy's order. Katy uses Fred's back for support to write the check!

"1500. Just like you said!"

Fred, a bit annoyed, whips around, "yes thank you."

Katy and Tommy drive back to the apartment. Katy can't believe that Manny would be involved!

"I think you said you went to see Manny, right?! Did you mention anything to him about your wrestling gig?!"

Katy turns a bit white, "I don't think I said what I was doing. But maybe just maybe I said I was going to the indoor soccer with Izzy. But now I'm not sure! My head is spinning."

Tommy tells her, "It's ok, relax. Just as Enzo said. We can be totally off here."

They get back to the apt and Tommy takes Izzy by the hand, "my dear you owe me at least a dinner and a movie for being your roommate's therapist and protector!"

"Maybe five minutes at the coffee shop on my way to work if you're lucky!" Izzy tells him and with that, she says "goodbye" and slams the door in his face!

Izzy turns to Katy, "ok that was a bit mean! I will pour the wine and you can fill me in on everything!"

Katy and Izzy are in the training ring at the lumberyard the following morning. Izzy whips Katy into the ropes! Izzy yells, "here comes the clothesline duck!"

Katy bounces off the ropes and gets hit with a clothesline square in the chest! Bam! She hits the mat hard! Izzy stands over Katy, "what was that?! Get your head in the game! Raquel will rip you apart plus I need you to push me to my limit so I can destroy Scarlet! So put all that worry on a shelf and focus! I need you!"

Just then Hannah strolls by the ring, "that's right Gargoyle Katy! You better stay on your back! Just let Raquel have her way with you! You do not want to even think about getting in the ring with me!" Hannah turns around and walks away!

Katy jumps to her feet and grabs Izzy! "Ok let's do this!"

They arrive home both tired and sore!

Izzy tells Katy that she can shower first.

"I need to rest a minute!"

Katy laughs, "you need to rest? You pinned me twice as much as I pinned you!"

"I don't know about that! It was great close battle!"

They both laugh then groan from the pain.

The next day Katy arrives at class moving a little slow. Upon seeing her, Tommy asks, "what happened to you?!"

Katy explains, "Izzy and I did some sparing to get ready for our next event."

With a big smile on his face, Tommy replies, "oh I would have loved to have seen that!"

"Be quiet Tommy. let's have a nice easy day of watching crime scene photos!"

After class Tommy asks Katy if she has heard from Manny.

"He called me, but I didn't pick up."

"Ok good." Tommy tells her. "The tox reports should be ready by now. Maybe no news is good news!"

Katy agrees. "Maybe but I really want to confront him."

"No way! That's a terrible idea! What if he is involved? Then he will know that you know. Please let's wait and see."

Reluctantly, Katy responds, "ok, but let's drop by and see Betty."

Tommy agrees, "But it will cost you a front row seat at the event so I can see my Izzy in action and cheer her on to victory. I will also cheer for you in your match!"

"Oh thanks", Katy tells Tommy. The response is dripping with sarcasm. "I can really feel the sincerity in that!"

Tommy giggles.

They head to the hospital and catch Betty as she is packing up to go home.

"Hooray you are on your feet!" Katy yells.

Betty asks, "are you ready for Raquel?!"

"Yes. Izzy whipped me into shape!"

"That's great. I'm sorry I won't be there, but I will be watching the livestream."

Tommy interrupts, "why? where are you going?"

Betty explains that her son is picking her up, "I will stay with him for a few days."

"That's nice. Get lots of rest." Katy tells Betty, "Because when I beat both Raquel and Hannah I wanna battle you for bragging rights!"

Betty laughs and gives Katy a hug.

"Just one more thing Betty. Is there anything at all from the attack that you might have missed?!" Katy is asking in a serious tone.

"Not that I can think of", Betty says. "But once I'm out of this place and have spent some quality time with my son I'm sure something will click, and you will be the first to know!" "Thank you, Betty."

"No! Thank you for being you! Now wipe the mat with Raquel!"

"Will do", Katy laughingly says.

It's the night of the special event. The electrician's union hall is hopping! Izzy and Katy are in the dressing room getting ready for battle. Somehow Tommy can pop his head in

"Izzy my dear I will be ringside screaming my head off for you!"

"Thanks Tommy, now beat it!" Izzy quickly yells as he is leaving, "only kidding, Tommy. I really do thank you!"

Katy and Izzy look over each other and have a big hug.

A lady comes in, "Isabelle it's time!"

"Snap her in two!" Katy exclaims.

"You got it!" Izzy yells back.

A short time later Katy hears the ring announcer says "….and this corner Isabelle the lady warrior Salinas!"

The crowd enthusiastically cheers! Katy finishes her hair and makeup and peeks at the ring from behind the entry curtain. She sees Izzy tying Scarlet O'Horror in knots! Izzy pounds away on Scarlett! This is it. Izzy has her trapped for the pin! But all of a sudden Scarlet's tag team partner Rebecca Rage jumps in and kicks Izzy off of Scarlet! Katy starts to run towards the ring when Brett grabs her arm. He says to wait and watch. Izzy pops up and levels Rebecca! The referee calls for the bell. Izzy throws both Rebecca and Scarlet out of the ring! The announcer says the winner of the match by disqualification is Isabelle the lady warrior Salinas! The crowd cheers!

Izzy takes the microphone, "Listen up Scarlet! This ain't over! I had you beat and I will do it again!"

The crowd chants "rematch! rematch!"

Izzy drops the mic and high fives Tommy as she jogs back to the dressing room! There she meets Katy who can't stop telling her how incredible it all was to watch.

"Yeah, it was ok." Izzy thanks her. "But now it's your turn! Tonight, you become a star!"

"Thank you, Izzy. I won't let you down!"

The lady now signals Katy to start walking towards the ring. Katy in her pink satin robe with white piping heads towards the ring!

The crowd cheers and says, "go get her Katy as she walks by."

Katy reaches the ring and hops on in. She gives a wave to the crowd! She removes her robe and she is wearing a tight hot pink one piece with white knee pads and shiny silver boots! The ring announcer takes the microphone and says "Ladies and Gentlemen this next match is to decide the number one contender for Hannah Glamour's crown! In this corner is the rookie sensation Gorgeous Katy!"

The crowd jumps up on their feet and cheer! Then he says "and in this corner the former two-time champion and a one-woman wrecking machine! The amazing Raquel Ruthless!"

The crowd boos and hisses!

They lock up! Raquel immediately goes for a rake of Katy's face but Katy slides to the right and quickly gets behind Raquel! Katy wraps her hands around Raquel's waist and arches backwards suplexing Raquel to the mat! Both the crowd and Raquel are in shock! They let out a cheer! But the joy doesn't last long as the match turns into a one-sided affair. Raquel is pummeling Katy and breaking every rule in the book! Tommy is in the first row with his hands over his face just barely peeking through his fingers. Next to him is Bobby and Becky Jasper with the look of sheer terror in their eyes! How is Katy hanging on?! It's one pin attempt after another with each time Katy coming closer to defeat! But then the crowd begins to stir. They are moved by Katy's sheer determination!

They start to chant "Katy! Katy!"

Raquel gets enraged and gets reckless! She jumps on the top rope and yells at the crowd to shut up! She then leaps off the top rope to finish Katy with a giant splash! But she took too long! Katy had just enough time to get her wits about her! She is still laying on the mat but gets her boots up just as Raquel is coming down! Wow! Raquel's chin slams right into Katy's boots! Raquel is knocked cold! But Katy is spent! The crowd stamps their feet and clap their hands giving Gorgeous Katy the energy she needs to crawl over and cover Raquel! Katy lays on the top of Raquel as the ref counts 1! 2!!......3!!!!!! Unbelievable! Katy did it!!

Izzy runs down the aisle and into the ring! She picks up Katy and both her and the referee raise her hands as the ringer announcer yells "In an amazing upset! The winner of the match is Gorgeous Katy!!"

The fans still can't believe it.

Raquel gets to her feet to unload on Katy but Izzy isn't having any of that! She shoves Raquel away! Raquel just rolls out of the ring in disgust! Katy blows kisses to the crowd as Izzy helps her back to the dressing room!

Izzy eases Katy into a chair.

Katy groans to Izzy, "Did that just happen or was I dreaming?

"No Katy you did it! Savor this moment! This is a once in a lifetime experience! Your first major upset of one of the best!"

Katy staggers to her feet and gives Izzy the warmest hug imaginable!

"Thank you, Isabelle! I owe this all to you!"

A few days had passed since the great victory. Katy gets into class.

Tommy looks up at her, "glad to see you are finally walking straight. That was some beating you took!"

Katy sternly replies, "I won, didn't I?! Now let's pay attention and maybe you will learn something. What's the topic today?"

"Police response to mass shootings I think." Tommy responds.

Just then Katy gets a text from Betty: call me ASAP!

Katy ducks out of the room and calls Betty.

"Slow down.", she tells Betty over the phone. "What was that? You saw the man's left hand?!"

"Yes, it was a white guy's hand," Betty is saying.

"You see a ring?! Or a scar or maybe a tattoo?!" Katy asks.

Betty replies, "no, definitely not."

"Ok, thank you and yes that was some match for sure!", Katy answers before hanging up the phone and returning to the classroom.

"Nice of you to join us Ms. Rachford, "Professor Enzo booms. "I hope you told the President that I said 'hi'".

After class, Katy grabs Tommy's hand and runs up to the Professor.

"Betty saw the attackers left hand!" Katy is yelling.

"And?!" Tommy quips.

"Nothing it had nothing on it!" Katy continues excitedly. "Manny has a giant stupid fraternity tattoo on his left hand! So, the attacker wasn't Manny. Also, it was a white guys hand."

"Well that really narrows it down!" Tommy says mockingly.

"Well, it's something.", the Professor interrupts. "But we still have no idea if the attack had anything to do with Brenda or Charlie. But here's what do know. Charlie's ex-wife! Guess who she married after him?! "

Tommy stares at the Professor, "who?! You?!"

"Not me, idiot. LT Toomey." Enzo further states, "…. Now, I'm really freaking interested. Maybe that's why the toxicology reports are so delayed and if they will ever actually see the light of day."

"Damn it!" Katy is frustrated. "This thing has so many tentacles. We need a real freaking break in this mess!"

Professor Enzo tries to soothe her, "alright, alright, alright! Let's relax. The key I believe is in the coroner's report. Cops may try to fudge things or hide things. But in all my years there have been very few coroners who will blatantly falsify their results. We just need to get those reports. We need a man on the inside. Or more accurately in this case a rookie indie circuit lady wrestler. Hey Katy ever do any undercover work?!

Tommy looks at the Professor in astonishment, "you got to be kidding!"

"I wish I was. But I think I can get an intern a temporary assignment there. Well Katy?! It's up to you?! We can give this a try, or we can just sit and wait until the police act or just move on."

Katy without hesitation says, "ok I will do it!"

"I knew I liked you! Ok let's get some hair dye and a fake ID!" the Professor says.

Katy and Tommy take their leave.

Tommy turns to Katy, "are you nuts?"

"Why?! Those guys aren't killers or corrupt they are Drs and lab techs."

Tommy snaps back, "I hope for your sake that's true."

Katy gets dropped off and walks in the apartment with a box of hair-dye that says Blissful Brunette. Izzy, with a concerned look on her face, says, "do I even want to know?!"

Katy laughs, "don't worry! I'm just going to work as an intern at the coroner's office for a bit." "And you need a disguise for that?!"

"My professor is just being overly cautious…. But oh yeah! Oh yeah! I spoke with Betty. She said she saw her attacker's left hand. No tattoo!"

Izzy is confused and asks Katy, "what are you taking about?"

Katy goes on to explain. "Manny has a big tattoo on his left hand, so her attacker wasn't him. But he still lied about all the problems he had with Brenda. So, we still got to be careful with him."

Izzy responds, now understanding. "Yes, we will be extra vigilant until this whole insane mystery is solved. But you're lucky Katy. Brett called me and said Hannah will be on vacation for a few weeks, so you don't have to make any appearances as a brunette Gorgeous Katy! I think you got her a bit nervous."

This makes Katy laugh. "She is probably getting Botox!"

Now Izzy bursts out in laughter!

Izzy composes herself and says, "but Brett asked if we could help his promoter friend out from a few towns away by being in a tag team match."

"But you just said I don't have to make any appearances with my brown hair!"

"Relax! Here is the best part." Izzy tells her friend. "We get to wear masks and be bad girls! We will be the Masked Miscreants! Tina and Tara Trouble!"

"Really?!" This could be a lot of fun Katy thinks to herself.

"Yeah! It will be so much fun! We will be taking on the Wholesome Twins Patience and Prudence! They just beat the snot out of the Taskmasters Carolina Day and Elena Palace." Izzy tells Katy.

Katy responds with "Oh I heard about the Taskmasters they are nasty! I'm glad they lost."

It's Katy's first day at the coroner's office. She has her newly light brown hair in a ponytail and she is wearing some horned rim glasses. She takes out her Fake ID with her new name Emily Byrnes and walks into the office where she is greeted by Dr Byron Brown, the coroner's office Deputy Director.

"Hello Miss Byrnes. I didn't think we were taking any more interns, but you came highly recommended by the mayor's office."

Katy thanks him, "sir I try to be a hard worker."

Dr Brown introduces Katy to Sarah Block, the head lab tech.

"Hi I'm Sarah." Sarah says extending a handshake to Katy.

"Nice to meet you, Sarah. I'm Emily Byrnes." Katy replies as she shakes Sarah's hand.

"I hope you're ready. We are going to have you dive right in."

"I'm ready! Let's go!"

Sarah brings Katy to the autopsy room.

"We normally don't let interns observe a procedure but if you do what you're told and really impress me I will see what I can do. But only if you want to. It's pretty intense! Now onto your job. It's paperwork, paperwork, paperwork. We carefully document every step in the process. Extensive notes and photos and lots of lab work. We keep paper copies of everything along with computer entry. "

Sarah points at Katy and says, "you never know if we will have to testify at a trial."

Katy listens intently as Professor Enzo discusses the differences between arson and an accidental fire. She looks over at Tommy who is doodling a picture of Izzy as a superhero. When the class ends Katy grabs Tommy and says, "come on, Stan Lee. Let's talk to Professor Enzo."

"Well miss brown haired girl how did it go?!" The Professor asks as Katy approaches. "I see you survived! I actually got some good feedback about you."

Katy is somewhat stunned. "Really?" she asks.

"Yeah. Now fill me in."

Katy sighs, "whoa there is a lot to it. I just kept my head down and took it all in. Next time I will start asking some questions."

"Ok but be careful" The Professor tells her. "Keep the questions very general like you are just trying to do your job better."

Katy nods, "yes good idea."

Tommy doesn't want to be left out of the action, "this is like mission impossible. What can I do?"

Enzo and Katy both look at Tommy and say, "we'll let you know!"

A sullen Tommy says "ok…. But I'd make a great secret agent."

Everyone laughs.

As they leave Mrs. Tobin, with a puzzled look on her face, sees them.

"Interesting new hairstyle, Miss. Rachford. Don't forget your next payment is coming up."

"Yes, ma'am I know."

"Very good. Fred keeps reminding me." Mrs. Tobin says.

Izzy and Katy arrive back at the apartment at the same time.

Tommy grins at Izzy, "oh Izzy I like the sweaty look on you."

"Zip it, Tommy. I just got finished working out."

Katy looks at Izzy, "you're a machine. Incredible!"

Izzy says, "yeah, yeah. Fill me in. How did it go?!" Then she turns to Tommy, "good night! See ya soon!"

Tommy pretends to tip his hat, "goodbye my ladies!"

Once inside the apartment, Katy starts to speak. "Wow! The coroner's office is a world unto itself."

"Oh I'm sure! But what did you find out?!"

"I'm just learning all the ins and outs. Soon I will do some poking around."

"Ok but be careful. Check these out!"

Katy turns to look, "what is that?!"

"Brett gave me our outfits for the match against the Wholesome twins."

Katy grabs a hanger, "oh cool! A scary black cat suit and matching mask!"

Izzy nods in agreement, "yeah, I'm so excited to play the role of a bad girl! Katy, it should be fun! We can blow off some steam and break the rules!". Katy laughs.

Katy feverishly works gathering documents and tracking all the incoming shipments. She even reorganizes their supply room. Then, after clearing off a desk, she takes a stack of papers in a folder labeled "finished" and walks over to Sarah.

"Sarah where exactly do the completed autopsy and toxicology reports go?"

"In the filing cabinet labeled 'ready for trial'. But let me see those, Emily. I'm glad you asked and didn't just try to file them away. These aren't completed yet.

"Oh, that's right. I'm so glad, Sarah, that you're my boss."

Sarah smiles and says thank you, "but we must be extra precise. While the police can lose their copies, we have to make sure we don't because they always come begging for another set. Let's head to the loading dock. The cute delivery guy is coming to drop off a shipment."

They both giggle!

Professor Enzo is trying to drive home the point that just because a body was pulled out of the water doesn't necessarily mean that they drowned.

Katy raises her hand, "is that why they check for water in the lungs?!"

Professor Enzo says, "yes, amongst other things. Very observant Ms. Rachford."

Tommy whispers "brown noser"

Katy just gives him a smug grin.

After class, Professor Enzo says to Katy, "so I guess you're learning a thing or two at the coroner's office."

"Yes! It's very interesting. But more importantly I was able to find out where they keep the toxicology reports. Next time I will try to make a copy."

"Ok. But be very, very careful. Don't rush it."

"Don't worry sir I will use my best judgment."

Tommy jumps in, "you dyed your hair and have a fake ID now. Maybe that's not the best choice. Just do the opposite of what you think you should do!"

Enzo says to Tommy, "this young lady has more guts and brains than anyone I know including you, Tommy!"

Katy says, "thank you sir. I try."

As they leave the classroom, they go the long way around to avoid Fred who keeps peeking his head out of the office.

"Are you coming to the match tonight?!", Katy asks Tommy.

"No. I still have some residual PTSD from watching you take a beating from that Raquel lady! Plus, my girl Izzy will be wearing a garbage bag with a mask over her face!"

Katy just shakes her head, "it's a cat suit not a garbage bag! But it's your loss!"

"Ok good luck and keep my Izzy safe!"

"Will do." Katy assures him.

Katy and Izzy keep peering in the mirror at the sight of themselves in black cat suits and matching masks.

"We look like two bad asses", she tells Izzy.

Izzy agrees, "Yeah, we do! Now let's be full on baddies!"

As they stroll to the ring under a cascade of boos.

Katy says to Izzy, "wow! They really hate us!"

"It sure seems like it."

They parade around the ring and see Bobby and Becky Jasper. Becky yells at a masked Katy, "I hope they squash you like a bug you tramp!"

Katy is taken back a bit but Izzy in full character goes up to Becky, "sit down and shut up you little brat!"

Becky turns white as a ghost and sits right down!

Katy and Izzy jump in the ring and the announcer declares, "….in this corner everyone's favorite darlings Patience and Prudence Wholesome!" The crowd cheers the two ladies dressed in white and gold looking like angels. Then he says, "….but in this corner are the masked miscreants! Tina and Tara Trouble!"

The crowd unloads on them with a hail of boos. The action gets right underway! The Wholesome twins are having a good time making the miscreants squirm. Patience has Katy wrapped up for the pin when Izzy comes flying in to save the match. The crowd groans in frustration! A short time later,. it's Izzy who is down and out. But Katy aka Tara gives Prudence a swift kick yet again keeping the Wholesome twins from winning the match.

Then the miscreants get really bad. They throw the rule book right out the window! Izzy has Patience in a headlock and drags her over to Katy.

Izzy yells at Katy!, "Hey Tara pay attention let's finish this."

Katy repeats, "sorry, sorry".

She comes in and slams Patience on the mat with a DDT! Katy hooks Patience's leg and pulls on her tights for extra leverage. The crowd yells that she is cheating as the referee counts 1! 2!! and 3!!! The ring announcer shouts, "the winners of the match are the masked miscreants!" Katy and Izzy dance around the ring to the boos of the crowd.

Back in the dressing room Izzy asks Katy, "what happened? You seemed distracted!"

"I don't know but I thought I saw someone who I used to know in the crowd and got an eerie feeling." Katy tells her.

"Ok we will stick together and have one of the security guys escort us to our car."

Katy looks at her phone and sees she has a missed call. She checks her messages and it's from Brenda's dad.

"Hello, Katy, this is Frank Chaplin Brenda's father. We finally got around to cleaning out her apartment and found her diary. I'm hoping we can meet up. There is something I need to show you."

Katy is a ball of nerves as she arrives at the coroner's office. She's never done anything like this before. If she gets caught, she would be arrested and could face jail time. She is going to make an unauthorized copy of the toxicology reports for both Brenda and Charlie.

Sarah walks up to Katy, "Emily are you feeling ok? You seem a little off."

"I'm ok Sarah I was just up all night with what I thought was a stomach bug. But don't worry. I tested myself. I'm Covid free."

"Ok, you've been doing a great job. Take it easy today. I have a meeting with Dr Brown so just do some easy filing until I get back."

"Thank you, Ms. Block."

Katy paces about and fidgets around shuffling some papers when she decides to go for it. Her heart is pounding so hard that she feels as if it will burst straight through her chest. She fumbles through the drawer and locates the folders. She takes a deep breath and goes to make some copies. Next thing you know, the copier shuts off! She is in a panic! But then she remembers the app on her phone to scan school papers. She quickly snaps a few shots then immediately puts everything away and slams the drawer!

"Emily what are you doing?!" Sarah asks.

Startled, Emily responds, "Nothing just organizing."

"Ok but Trooper Garner has been waiting to get a copy of the toxicology report from the fatal car accident."

Katy lets out a huge sigh of relief, "hello Trooper Garner. I will get that for you right now."

Back in class Professor Enzo goes on and on about how a man killed six women over a three-year period using icicles. Tommy looks over at Katy and he can see the wheels spinning in her head. She is deep in thought. He waves at her to no avail. Professor Enzo looks up and sees Tommy waving his hand.

"Mr Getter! Do we have a mosquito problem in here?"

"What? No! I was just…." Tommy stutters.

Shaking his head, "Forget it. Just pay attention." The Professor says.

After class, Professor Enzo sees Tommy and Katy racing towards him.

"Oh boy! It's the wonder twins! So, what cha got?!"

"Here! Here! Look!", Katy tells him, waiving her phone at him.

He takes her phone and scrolls through saying "blah blah heroin. Blah blah Xanax blah blah Zoloft. Nothing here. I don't see a connection. Both causes of death undetermined."

Katy pleads desperately "please keep looking!"

Enzo goes through again and then his eyes start to bulge "What?! No way!"

"What?! What is it?!" Katy begs.

The Professor tells her, "Lab tech Block wrote on the very bottom of both tox reports minute possibility of Phyllobates Terribilis? "

"What is that?!" Tommy asks.

Professor Enzo yells "Doesn't anyone pay attention in my class?! It's the Golden Poison Dart Frog! The most poisonous frog in the world! Why the hell do they both have that on their reports?! Strange things are afoot at the Circle K!"

Katy and Tommy look at him in bewilderment.

"Bill and Ted's Excellent Adventure! Before your time! But these poor people got murdered!", the Professor explains.

Katy sobbingly says "I knew it! Now what?!"

"Now I gotta think. Did the cops just miss that? Is Sarah Block crazy? Are they trying to cover it up?! Great job Katy! But I'm going to have to make some calls. Class dismissed!"

Katy and Tommy leave class and blow right past Fred as he tries to stop them.

"Not now, Fred! Talk to you tomorrow!"

Katy gets home and yells "Izzy! Izzy! Brenda was murdered!"

"What?!" Izzy yells back.

"Yes! Some exotic frog poison"

"Frog poison?! This is some tin foil hat wearing conspiracy stuff."

"I have a strange feeling about this. Something about this seems familiar."

"Whoa. Alright let's relax and have a drink to calm your nerves." Izzy tells Katy, "Did you go see Brenda's dad? How did that go?"

Katy's eyes widen as she says "oh no! I will call him right now."

Katy makes the call and tells Izzy she will meet with Mr. Chaplin first thing tomorrow.

"Ok Katy. Let's do a shot then I have some news for you!"

They both slam down a shot of Fireball and Izzy declares, "Hannah Glamour is back in town, and she is looking to beat you so bad that you won't ever even utter the word wrestling again!"

Katy sighs, "when is this supposed to happen?"

"Brett is working that out now! I will also have a huge No DQ match with Scarlet O'Horror!" It's time for you to go back to being a blonde beauty!"

Katy laughs, "yes! Yes, it is!"

Katy is up early and makes a call to the coroner's office, "hello Ms Block this is Emily Byrnes. I really appreciated the opportunity to work with you and all the fine Doctors at the Coroner's office. But I'm too swamped with all my other responsibilities. I'm so sorry but I won't be coming back."

"Oh, Emily I understand. This isn't for everyone, but my door will always be open to you." "Thank you so much Sarah that means a lot."

Katy hangs up the phone. "Ok time to meet Mr. Chaplin", she thinks to herself.

Katy arrives at the Diner and sees Mr. Chaplin sitting in a booth just staring into his cup of coffee. Katy sits down across from him, "I'm so sorry about Brenda! I didn't know her for that long but in the time we had she was very special."

Mr. Chaplin responds, "thank you very much. Apparently, you made quite the impression on her as well. Please read this."

Mr Chaplin hands Katy Brenda's diary. Katy reads a few passages.

One says "I met two cool people in my reality of crime class. Silly Tommy and this lady Katy. She is amazing. So strong and confident. She always has all the answers. She is smart as a whip."

The second one says "Katy is in training. I can't believe it. I'd never be so bold as to try something like that. I can't wait to go to her first match!"

The last one says "I don't know what to do. I was going to see T. because Dr. Sanjay never gives me enough Xanax. I heard this guy asking all these questions to all these people about Katy. Maybe he's an old friend but I got a bad feeling about him. I hope he didn't realize that I heard what he was saying."

Katy's heart sinks.

Mr. Chaplin asks, "are you a tennis player or something? Do you think this T. guy had anything to do with Brenda's overdose?!"

"No sir I don't play tennis. But can I have her diary? I will make sure this whole thing gets investigated thoroughly and if anyone did anything to Brenda they will be brought to justice. But for now sir all I want to say is I'm so sorry for your loss and Brenda was a great friend." Mr. Chaplin says "thank you Katy. I can see my Brenda was right about you!"

Tommy is slumped over the desk barely conscious. Professor Enzo goes over which power tool is the one most widely used by the Mafia to cut up bodies. As Tommy's torment ends Katy gets right into it with Professor Enzo. She shows him Brenda's diary. Katy points out the passage about a guy asking questions.

The Professor asks, "anyone have any reason to hate you, Katy?"

"No. The break up with Manny went ok. I think he still likes me. Plus, he wasn't the one who attacked Betty! I will have to really think about that one."

Not totally convinced, Professor Enzo says, "Alright. But in other news. I had it out with LT. Toomey. He showed me the toxicology reports that Det. Franklin had and in his copy, there was no mention of the frog poison. You must have gotten a copy of a preliminary report and the coroner's office probably made Ms. Block remove it because it was so out of the realm of possibility. I have some information on LT Toomey that would be highly Detrimental to any future political campaign which I am seriously considering using now."

"Ok what do we do now?", Katy asks Professor Enzo.

"You wanna catch this guy, right?"

An emphatic "Absolutely!" from Katy.

"Then Katy we will have to use you as bait to catch this guy!"

"No way! Too dangerous!" Tommy cries.

"No, no I will do it. What's your plan?" Katy insists.

Professor Enzo asks "do you have a big match coming up or something? Something that we can use?"

"Yes! My big match with Hannah Glamour!"

"Perfect! Get the word out that you will be out front early to talk to the fans and take pictures. If this guy really hates you he won't be able to resist ruining your special day! I will force Toomey and Franklin to set a trap!"

"Thank you, sir I will do it!" Katy grins.

In the apartment, Katy gets Izzy up to speed on the latest plan.

"I should slap you silly! My poor mother will have prayed nonstop for a month to keep you safe on this one!"

Katy gives Izzy a hug, "don't worry, Izzy, between your mom praying and the police looking out I will be fine! But how can we get the word out about the match?"

"Leave that to me! There is this dude, Vinny. He's a magician and a wrestling fan who has a podcast. He owes me a favor. We can talk about our matches on his show!"

The next ten days are filled with long training sessions and school projects. Izzy and Katy tie each other up in knots as they push themselves to be ready for the challenges ahead.

The day of the podcast, Katy and Izzy arrive at Vinny's house and his mom directs them down to the basement.

Izzy is choking on all the magic trick smoke, "Vinny please knock it off for a bit!"

He reluctantly agrees and motions them to a seat, "sit on down and get comfortable."

Then he sits in his gaming chair and flips a switch, "hello my people! Welcome to your favorite podcast, Vinny the Virtuoso's Rasslin Hour! I'm your host Vinny the Virtuoso and man, do I have a treat for you!"

Vinny winks at Izzy and says, "let's welcome my girl Isabelle The Lady Warrior Salinas and her new tag team partner and rookie sensation Gorgeous Katy!"

Katy says, "hello wrestling fans I'm thrilled to be here and honored to be Izzy's tag team partner!"

Izzy chimes in, "no Katy! I'm the one who is honored!"

Vinny says, "so tell me about your huge upcoming matches!"

Izzy jumps right in, "I'm taking on that no good cheating loser Scarlet O'Horror and her tag team partner Rebecca Rage better not interfere, or I will flatten her!"

"Damn! Look out Scarlet! Izzy is on a mission!" Vinny comments

"That's right!" says Izzy. "Now let's talk about Katy! She is taking on Hannah Glamour for the ladies' championship! This will be the greatest night of Katy's career without a doubt! I want everyone to come out to the Arena and cheer Katy onto victory! We will also have a special treat for the fans who get there early! Gorgeous Katy will be out front talking to the fans and taking selfies!"

"Don't you dare miss it!" Vinny says. He continues, "wow Katy! Hannah has wrestled all over the world and doesn't like to lose! I hope you're ready! You look more like a lady who should be teaching Sunday school than getting in the ring with Hannah! But I wish you the best of luck! I want all my fans to head out to the Arena and witness history in the making!"

It's the day of the championship event. A small crowd has gathered by the athlete's entry tunnel to the Arena. LT. Toomey and Detective Franklin are doing a terrible job trying to blend in with the crowd. Katy and Izzy are there laughing and talking with the fans and taking selfies!

Hannah Glamour walks by and says "really? You people want to talk to her? I'm the star! I'm the champion! You're all pathetic!" Hannah then saunters off into the tunnel.

"Please don't listen to her! I appreciate you all. I love you guys!", Katy tells her fans.

The small group cheers!

Franklin and Toomey keep walking around and staring at people up and down. But nothing has happened.

Izzy turns to Katy that "it's time to go!"

Katy blows the group some kisses, "see you inside. Wish me luck!"

As they start down the tunnel a man in a hooded sweat shirt runs straight through the crowd making a bee line towards Katy!

Detective Franklin yells "Stop! Police!"

Then he tases the hooded man! LT Toomey knocks the man to the ground. Izzy runs over and gives him a kick! She then yanks down his hood as Detective Franklin keeps hitting the tase button! They roll him over and Katy sees that it's Fred from school.

"Fred, you want me dead?" Katy asks, stunned.

Fred stutters from the shocking "No! No! I came to give you an overdue bill! Here! Here it is!" LT Toomey yells "you're an idiot! You could have gotten yourself killed!"

Fred again stutters, "giving people bills is my job!"

Katy laughs and makes her way into the tunnel.

Then from out of the darkness a black glove covers her mouth. She tries to scream but can't! All she sees is the gleam of a needle as it plunges towards her neck! She closes her eyes waiting for it to be all over! Then BAM! A gun shot! Her ears ring as the gloved man hits the floor! She is disoriented but sees Professor Enzo kick the needle away and shove a gun in the masked man's mouth! She gathers her wits and begs Professor Enzo to stop as he begins to slowly squeeze the trigger! He turns and sees the goodness in her eyes and pulls the gun out of the man's mouth.

Katy yanks off the man's mask, "I know you! You're Kurt Mauer's brother! He was one of the guys who raped my friend!"

The man responds, "Yes! You ruined his life and I want you to die! You better sleep with one eye open! There will be more of us! We will get you!"

The Professor steps on the man's shoulder wound and as the man screams Enzo says "shut up! You're done! Your friends are done!" Then he yells "Franklin! Toomey! Get the hell over here!"

Izzy runs up in a panic and hugs Katy!

"Oh my God! Are you ok?! Are you ok?!"

"Yes! I am now! Thank you, Professor!" Katy says as she looks over at Professor Enzo.

Softly, the Professor, says "Katy, Call me Ray. I'm glad you're ok. Now don't you have a fight to win? They will get your statement later."

Izzy clamors "Yes! Yes, we do!" Then she starts to drag Katy inside!

Enzo yells after them, "go get 'em girls! We will clean this mess up!"

Izzy takes Katy into the dressing room "that's it! I'm telling Brett that your match is off! You've been through too much!"

Katy gently grabs Izzy's shoulders, "aren't you the one who said never to let fear stop you?! Well, it's not going to stop me!"

Izzy with tears in her eyes hugs Katy "you're so amazing! Let's do this!"

Katy responds with a "Hell yeah!"

They get all dressed up. Their suits and make up look perfect.

Tommy runs into the dressing room in a panic, "what the hell happened? It's a zoo outside!" Izzy barks at Tommy, "we are fine! Now go to your seat and I better see you cheering your head off for me!"

Tommy nervously laughs and dashes away!

A lady walks in and motions for Izzy to head to the ring! Izzy gives Katy a high five then runs through the curtain!

As she leaves Brett Rodgers the wrestling company owner walks in and over to Katy, "My God are you ok? I only got a little bit of info from the cops but holy cow! Listen, I know this is a big match but there will be others, the choice is yours. If you're not 100 percent, I totally understand."

"Thank you, sir, but I'm ok I'm ready!", Katy assures him.

"Ok good! Now Hannah is a killer. So, there is absolutely no shame in defeat. You stepped up when no one else would! In my opinion you're a champion no matter what!"

"Oh, thank you."

At that moment, Katy can hear a ton of loud boos coming from the ring! She rushes to the curtain and sees Rebecca Rage holding Izzy as Scarlet O'Horror pounds away on her!

Katy yells "no! Izzy is in trouble! They are double teaming her and they won't get disqualified!"

Katy runs out from the back and gets halfway down the aisle when from out of nowhere comes Betty Bass! Betty flies into the ring and nails Rebecca upside the head with an elbow strike! The crowd goes crazy as she body slams Rebecca to the mat then kicks her out of the ring!

Betty yells at Izzy "You got Scarlet, girl! Take her out!" as she dives through the ropes tackling Rebecca!

Izzy, with fire in her eyes, scoops up a charging Scarlet using her momentum against her slams Scarlet to the mat! Bam! Scarlet hits the mat hard! Izzy runs and springs off the ropes! Wow! She nails Scarlet with a knee to the forehead! Izzy pounces on Scarlet and goes for the pin! The ref counts 1! 2!! but oh! Scarlet kicks out! She pops up and pokes her thumb in Izzy's eye! She gives Izzy a chop to the chest then whips Izzy into the ropes! Izzy bounces off as Scarlet goes for a clothesline! Izzy ducks it and catches Scarlet in a crucifix hold! Izzy takes Scarlet to the mat! Scarlet is trapped! Her shoulders are down! The ref counts 1! 2!! 3!! Izzy did it! Izzy wins! The referee raises her hand as the ring announcer proclaims, "the winner of this thrilling match is Isabelle the Lady Warrior Salinas!"

The crowd goes wild!!

Tommy is on his feet screaming and yelling "I love you Izzy!"

Izzy gets to the back and is greeted by Betty!

Izzy looks at Betty, "boy! You showed up just at the right time! I was in trouble!"

Betty says "of course! You girls are the best you guys saved my life!"

Then Izzy and Betty turn to Katy.

Izzy says "we love you! We are here for you! This is your night! Go out there and win!"

Katy with tears in her eyes hugs them both, "I haven't had friends like you two ever! Thank you so much! I'm going to make you two proud!"

The lady signals Katy to head to the ring.

Katy turns and faces Izzy and Betty, "here we go! Izzy, call your mom! Ask for one more prayer!" She then heads out towards the ring! The second the crowd sees her they go insane! She gets cheers and high fives and hugs all the way to the ring! She hops up and gives the crowd a wave!

They chant "Katy! Katy! Katy!"

Then the ring announcer says, "ladies and gentlemen this is the main event of the evening! This match is for the Ladies Championship Belt! In this corner is the challenger and the darling of the wrestling world! Let's hear it for Gorgeous Katy!"

The crowd again chants "Katy! Katy! Katy!"

"And in this corner a lady who is known worldwide. It's the Ladies Champion The beautiful! The fearless! The spectacular Hannah Glamour!!"

The crowd boos as Hannah calls them all ugly slobs!

The bell rings and the two ladies go right at it! Hannah charges Katy but she drops down and grabs a hold of Hannah's wrist! Katy arm whips Hannah to the mat! The crowd cheers! Hannah jumps right up and snap kicks Katy square in the chest! Katy flies backwards into the ropes! Hannah charges nailing Katy in the midsection with a knee! Hannah keeps Katy trapped against the ropes and unloads on her with a series of knee strikes and forearm smashes! Hannah starts choking Katy until the referee finally makes her break the hold! Katy falls to the mat coughing!

Hannah parades around the ring yelling "I'm the champion! She is pathetic!"

The match continues and Hannah puts on a wrestling clinic showing exactly why she is the

champion! Katy has the heart of a lion but even her biggest fans can see this won't end well for her! Every time Katy starts to gain a little steam Hannah slams the door shut. Hannah picks up Katy and power bombs her to the mat! She leaps up and hits Katy with a double leg drop! Hannah does a fashion pose on top of Katy as the ref counts 1! 2!! Thr…!!

What?! Did Katy get her shoulder up?! Yes! Yes, she did! Hannah is livid! She picks up Katy and whips her into the ropes! Whoa! Hannah nails Katy with a drop kick! Katy is on the mat holding her face! Hannah rolls Katy over and again goes for the pin! Some people in the front row yell "stay down Katy! Stay down!" As the ref counts 1! 2! and a kick out! Katy kicks out! Hannah pounds the mat in frustration! The crowd applauds Katy's valiant effort. Hannah picks Katy up and slaps her across the face! Katy staggers back then strikes Hannah with a forearm smash! The crowd couldn't believe it! They trade blows in the center of the ring! Hannah goes to whip

Katy into the ropes! But Katy reverses it! Hannah goes and bounces off the ropes! Katy goes for a clothesline, but Hannah dodges it and springs off the opposite side! She goes to hit Katy with a high cross body block! But Katy drops to the mat! Hannah flies through the air and crashes to the mat knocking the wind right out of her! Katy runs and attempts to scoop Hannah up for a body slam! But whoa! Hannah wraps up Katy in a small package! The ref counts 1! 2!! 3!!! No! No! Somehow Katy kicked out! You can't get any closer than that! Hannah is beside herself! Hannah picks up Katy and goes for a body slam! But Katy slips out of it and is behind Hannah! Katy shoves Hannah into the ropes! They fall backwards!Katy rolls on top of Hannah! Hannah is folded in half! Katy does a backwards bridge! Hannah is trapped. The ref is stunned!

Katy screams "count her already"

So the ref counts 1! 2!! ....3!!!!! Unbelievable! Incredible!! Impossible!! But it's true! The ref raises a still completely shocked Katy's hand as the fans are going wild.

"In one of the biggest upsets in wrestling history the winner of the match and NEW Ladies Champion is Gorgeous Katy!!"

Katy asks for the microphone, "thank you all so much! I love you all, but I could not have done this without Isabelle Salinas and Betty Bass!"

Just as Katy is speaking, both Izzy and Betty jump into the ring and swarm her!

Katy continues to say "and a huge thank you to Hannah Glamour! You're an incredible wrestler! I wanted to give up several times! You're a true legend I'm so so lucky to have survived let alone get the win!"

The crowd applauds Katy's genuine humility. Even Hannah gives a reluctant clap!

Back in the dressing room Katy, Izzy and Betty laugh and cry!

Katy says in awe, "this has been the most surreal day of my life!"

Just then Professor Enzo walks in, "are you ladies decent?"

They laughed, "yes!", in unison.

"Wow Katy incredible! I didn't see it, but I heard it!" The Professor states. "Let me fill you all in on all that has just happened! Kent Mauer, the guy who tried to kill you Katy and you Betty, *"Graciously"* gave a full confession stating he was part of some BS Aryan and anti-women society. When their brothers and friends were arrested for the rape of Katy's friend, they made a pact to eliminate Katy! He came to town to do just that. He killed Charlie Bruen as a sick experiment to test the poison. He then killed poor Brenda because he was worried that she might have heard too much!"

Katy asks, "Why go after Betty?!"

Enzo explains "the fool thought it was you. But Betty was too damn tough!"

"But where did they get the poison from?!" Izzy asks.

The Professor tells them, "One of their members learned about it when he was in the army stationed in South America!"

"That's so sick!" Katy says. She is still worried. "But are they still going to come after me?!" The Professor smiles "don't you worry about that Katy! I have some "friends" in Brooklyn who are going to head out west and politely ask them to leave you alone while they are dangling upside down over the side of a bridge! So, I can guarantee that problem is solved!" "Professor Enzo! I mean Ray! I can't thank you enough!" Katy beams.

Ray smiles again, "No Katy! I must thank you! My faith in mankind has been restored. You are the smartest, bravest, and most loyal lady I have ever met! Now go find Tommy he will want to see this circus of a press conference!"

A short time later they all gather outside of the arena where there is a podium and a microphone set up. LT Toomey steps up to the microphone and gives a statement to the press. "Thank you all for coming. I'm LT Toomey. I've been in charge and have been spearheading this entire investigation. Since I first learned about the death of Charlie Bruen I've been doing nothing else. Then once we learned about the murder of Ms. Brenda Chaplin and the attempted murder of Miss Betty Bass. It's been all hands on deck. I'd like to thank Detective Franklin for his excellent crime scene work that discovered the poison used in these crimes. Between the two of us we planned the sting operation that led to the arrest of the subject. The rumors about one of the competitors in tonight's event ever being in danger are completely false! Now many years ago I made a pledge as an officer to keep the people safe. I have fulfilled that pledge. So it is on that note that I will be retiring from the police department. But I would be honored to again serve the good people of this fine community by being elected a member of the city council. So as my last act as commander of the Detective division I'm formally promoting Detective Franklin to be my replacement. I thank you all for your time."

Katy, Tommy, Betty, and Isabelle are left with their mouths wide open in total disbelief! Ray just laughs saying "that my friends is your final lesson on the reality of crime!"

Eighteen months later, Katy is in her new office. The temporary sign on the door reads" Katy Rachford Forensic Psychologist and Private Investigator." She is waiting for the permanent one to arrive. She is at her computer reading an email from Tommy. He is a forever student now enrolled in medical school. He wants to be a pediatrician just like his mom. He sends a pic of himself in a lab coat wearing an I love Izzy the lady warrior tee shirt! Katy laughs then clicks on a wrestling article. Isabelle Salinas has been taking the Canadian wrestling scene by storm! Katy says to herself "you go Izzy!"

Just then a well-dressed middle-aged woman walks in.

Flustered, she addresses Katy, "I think my ex husband was murdered and no one wants to help!" Katy does a fourth wall break and smiles!

"Let's get it started" by The Black Eyed Peas begins to play!

RACHFORD PRIVATE EYE

Fall is in the air bringing all sorts of new changes.

As Katy Rachford unpacks her things in her new office, she admires her desktop name plate: "Katy Rachford Private Investigator".

She leans back in her chair and reflects on all that has transpired over the past year, smiling as she thinks back on getting justice for Brenda and helping to put away that monster. She laughs remembering her roller coaster wrestling career. The laugh turns into a sigh as she misses her good friend Izzy who is up in Canada becoming an arctic wrestling superstar! She even misses wacky Tommy who is now enrolled in Medical School!

"But it's all good! Look at me now! Katy Rachford Private Eye", she exclaims! as Ray Enzo walks in, "Take it easy there Sherlock Holmes! You have lots to learn before you get your pipe and magnifying glass! It's still the Raymond Enzo Private Investigation Firm! You will be boss soon enough!"

Katy laughs, "I know! I know! I'm just so excited about this opportunity!"

"That's great! But we must learn to crawl before we can run!"

"I will take lots of notes and pay close attention!"

"I know you will. That's why you are here! I have complete faith in you!"

Ray is proud of Katy. She is a new age vigilante. Katy wants to help the single mother get the proper child support from the absentee father. She wants to stop fraudsters from scamming the tax payers with their false claims. She wants to expose the lying and cheating husbands who don't respect their wives! She wants to help those who the system has discarded! She wants to make a difference!

Later that evening, Katy meets up with her old friend from the Air Force, Jenny Ryan. On her way to meet Jenny, Katy reflects. She is happy to have recently reconnected with Jenny who just went through a bad divorce and is glad Jenny accepted the invitation to share the apartment above her office. Hopefully, the new job Jenny just started as an entry level position as a billing processor for the local power company will help her get back on her feet.

"So? How did it go?" Katy asks as she sits down with Jenny at the table.

"I think I will fit right in. The pay is a bit low but hopefully over time that will improve."

"That's good! I'm glad you came and I'm glad you took the job. Just stick with it and the pay will come."

"Thank you! Do you need any help with setting up your office?"

"I think I got it. Now all I need is some juicy cases to investigate!"

"I know they will come, Katy. People flock to you when they are in need!"

Bright and early the next morning an elderly lady comes into Katy's office. She is obviously distressed. "Hello, my name is Harriet Hamilton. I can't find my dog anywhere. Please help."

"I can call the pound for you. That's not what I really do but I can start there." Katy answers.

"I tried that. I really need my Chester back," Harriet wails.

"Leave me a picture and your phone number and I will see what I can do." "Oh, thank you! Thank you!" Harriet exclaims.

Later that afternoon as Katy is cooking pasta, Jenny comes home.

"I got my first big case!" Katy blurts out.

"Oh yeah?! That's great! What's the caper?!" Jenny replies with a hint of amusement sneaking into her voice.

"Lost dog!" Katy giggles.

"Well, it's a start!" Jenny laughingly proclaims. "I got to issue a final notice for nonpayment on somebody", she continues proudly.

"Wow! "We have the most exciting lives," Katy counters, feigning her best sarcastic tone.

Jenny laughs, "But speaking of excitement, my boss gave me two tickets to the pro wrestling show at the VFW. His son got in trouble at school, so he gave the tickets to me instead."

"Wow ok! That's Kevin King's promotion. He is a nice guy. But I didn't know you were into that, Jenny."

"Ever since I saw that YouTube video of you beating Hannah Glamour I was hooked! You were incredible, Katy!"

Katy laughs "Yeah that was great! But in our rematch, she won!"

Jenny grabs Katy's hands, "What?! That rematch was amazing! You had her beat yet again when her stupid sister Savannah helped Hannah cheat! That's the only reason why she won! Everyone saw that!"

"Yeah, I guess." Katy says with a sigh.

Katy and Jenny have a front row seat for all the action at the VFW. They cheer and boo! They get into it and enjoy the excitement and drama! Next thing you know this red-headed lady wearing a bright green suit comes out. It's Shannon Star the former ladies champion of Kevin King's wrestling group.

She looks at Katy and Jenny "Who are you two pathetic losers?! What? Neither one of you can get a man?" Then she does a double take and says "wait a minute! You're Gorgeous Katy! You better not even think about wrestling for my group!"

The crowd boos as Shannon struts away and hops in the ring! She goes on to destroy Sadie Shaker much to the dismay of the crowd. After the event Kevin King, the owner of the small wrestling association, stops Katy and Jenny, "I was watching you two. You have good chemistry! Are you sisters?!"

"No, we are good friends from the Air Force." Katy answers.

"You're Gorgeous Katy! I saw you wrestle". Kevin proclaims. "The fans absolutely love you! But who is your friend? I think you two would make a great tag team. Is she a wrestler?"

Jenny quickly states, "No sir but I'd love to learn!"

"Great! Katy, I can pay you to train your friend here…. I'm sorry I didn't get your name." Kevin says as he eyes Jenny up and down.

"I'm Jenny Ryan."

"Great! I will pay you and Jenny to learn the ropes in the evenings if you like?! Give it a week or two. Try it out."

Although a bit hesitant, Katy speaks up first. She doesn't want to be insulting but at the same time, isn't quite comfortable with the idea, "I'm so busy with my new job and Jenny just got into town but maybe in the future though."

Jenny flashes Katy a look of disappointment and begins to utter when Shannon Star comes out from the back wearing jeans and a NYC hoodie, "those two losers?! Ha! Katy was a flash in the pan and her friend looks like a wimp! They won't do it!"

With color rising in her checks, Katy looks directly into Jenny's eyes and, as if they are reading each other's minds, they declare in unison "Ok two weeks! Let's see what happens."

As Shannon storms off, Kevin smiles a toothy grin and happily shouts "Alright!! You ladies just made my night!"

It's a slow morning and Katy is at her desk putting pins on a map of possible places where a stray dog might go. She turns towards the door when she hears it open and sees Jimmy Adams, the star quarterback for the high school football team, entering her office. In his arms, he is carrying a small white dog.

"Hello ma'am I saw this guy just wandering in the street. I didn't want him to get hit by a car and I saw your office open. Can you call the pound? I'm late for school."

"Sure ok!", Katy exclaims as she retrieves the dog from Jimmy's arms.

She reads the tag on his collar and laughs. Could it be?

"Oh, Chester you just made my day! Let me call your mom!"

After the successful closing of the Mischievous Missing Maltese, Ray walks in and says, "Excellent work there, private eye!" I have a lady here that I want you to talk to."

He is followed by a very well-dressed lady whom he introduces as Jill Silverman.

"It's nice to meet you Ms. Rachford. Ray here tells me you are a very well respected up and coming private eye. I am hoping you can help me."

"I certainly will try my best."

"I think my low-down dirty husband Justin is cheating on me," Mrs. Silverman starts to explain.

"Ok come in and sit down." Katy says and just motions to a chair, "please tell me why you think that."

Mrs. Silverman goes on to describe how he stays out late during the week and must run out to the office late at night sometimes on the weekends. She further states that his clothes smelled like a perfume that wasn't hers.

Katy contemplates Mrs. Silverman's words for a moment, looks at Ray and tells her, "Hmm give me the address of his office and the type of car he drives. I will talk it over with my boss and I will let you know how we will want to proceed."

Satisfied with this response, Mrs. Silverman hires Katy and its onto case #2 for Katy Rachford Private Investigator!

It's day one of training. Katy meets up with Jenny at Kevin King's training facility.

"I cracked my first case." Katy tells Jenny.

Jenny gives Katy a bewildered look, "Oh yeah? What? How? Who?"

Katy laughs "I found the dog! Or more accurately the dog found me."

They both giggle.

Then Jenny asks in a more serious tone, "are you ready? Are we really going to try this?"

"Am I ready? You're the one who wants to give it a try! But we don't have to if you're having second thoughts!"

Jenny instantly counters and says "no! I'm ready! Let's see what happens. I might love it or I might leave here on a stretcher!".

They both let out a hearty laugh. It's good. It relieves some tension they didn't even realize was there.

As they walk through the door, they are immediately greeted by Wendy Wakeford a longtime independent pro wrestler and good friend of Kevin King.

"Wow! Gorgeous Katy! It's a pleasure to meet you! And you must be the Marine Corps girl." Wendy states and she gives a light-hearted acknowledgement salute to the pair.

"Prior Air Force," Jenny gently corrects.

"Same thing. You're a hero." Wendy says as she escorts Katy and Jenny into a room with a bunch of mats and a wrestling ring.

There, they are greeted by Sandy Straight an up-and-coming lady wrestler who is training for a wrestling tour in Japan!

Wendy asks Katy if she wants to roll around with Sandy a bit to shake the cobwebs loose while she gets Jenny started.

Katy graciously accepts with a "oh yes thank you! Let's go Sandy!"

Katy and Sandy show each other some new tricks while Jenny is being put through the ringer by Wendy! Katy and Sandy are trading holds when they hear a loud boom! They run over and see Jenny on the mat with the wind knocked out of her!

"Are you ok, Jenny?!" Katy asks.

Wendy replies "She is fine! She just got a bit overzealous while jumping off the top rope!" Katy yells "Jenny! You can't learn it all in one day! It takes time."

A very sore, winded Jenny gasps out "ok, ok, I see that now!"

Katy lifts Jenny up by the arms, saying "come on champ! Let's go home!"

The following morning Katy is up and ready to take on the world! Jenny is moaning and groaning slamming down 4 Advil with her coffee but manages to mutter "have A great day; I hope to be leaving soon."

Katy chuckles, looking back over her shoulder at Jenny as she walks out the door, "don't worry it gets easier!"

First thing, Katy heads to Ray's office. She wants to get advice on how to catch Justin Silverman cheating.

"Katy, you need to take it slow. I will go out with you and teach you how to surveil a subject. Then if it is necessary I will show you how to tail a vehicle."

Katy pays close attention and takes lots of notes! Over the next few weeks, the days are filled with a mix of taking videos and snapshots along with documenting lots of suspicious activities. Katy meticulously gathers all the dirt on Justin. For Jenny, it is working diligently at the power company. This works out well for her and she gets a bump in pay for closing out all the overdue invoices. But at night Katy, Wendy, and Sandy pass along

THE ADVENTURES OF GORGEOUS KATY

their knowledge of ring tactics to Jenny! They constantly lend support to Jenny as she struggles but gives it her all!

"I know Kevin wants you guys to be a tag team", Wendy tells Katy and Jenny, "But I really feel Jenny's first match should be a one-on-one contest against another girl."

Katy agrees.

"Let's give you a ring name Jenny!", Wendy continues. She reiterates that this is very important and tells Jenny, "I've talked it over with Katy and we have given this a lot of thought. We feel that you and Katy are elegant ladies who play by the rules. So, your tag team name will be Team Elegance."

Jenny, in a bit of a disenchanted voice says, "oh that's nice, but what about my individual name?!"

"Jenny you're not afraid to take risks in the ring and love to fly through the air! You also handle defeat with dignity. Your ring name is Jet-Set Jenny Ryan!"

Jenny's voice perks up "oh I like that!"

Wendy continues in dramatic style with her arms outstretched in front of her, "I can see it up in lights now. Jet-Set Jenny Ryan and Gorgeous Katy! Team Elegance."

Back in Ray's office, Ray marvels," damn Katy! I've haven't seen such a well put together case in quite a while. I think it's time to give Mrs.,

Silverman a call!" A short time later Jill Silverman arrives. Katy sits her down and lays out all the evidence that they have gathered on Justin.

After listening to the details of proof gathered, an extremely agitated Mrs. Silverman satisfactorily asserts, "that lying, cheating, son of a bitch! I'm going to take him for every penny that I can!"

In a sincere tone, Katy tells Mrs. Silverman, "I'm terribly sorry that it had to be this way, but we thoroughly investigated everything a few times over to be absolutely sure."

Mrs. Silverman looks at Katy and replies, "Don't be sorry, you did what I asked. Thank you so much. I can see all the hard work that you put into this!"

She then turns to Ray and says, "Mr. Enzo you have one hell of an investigator here!"

"Yes! She is quite the prodigy!", beams Ray,

Once the office door closes behind Mrs. Silverman, Ray looks to Katy.

"Great job Katy! Now I can go away to upstate NY deer hunting with my old crew!'

"Ok I will hold down the fort."

"No! No! No! I'm going to be out of cellphone range and will only check my messages every so often. You just take names and information! Don't do anything until I get back!"

"Ok that's all I will do!", Katy smirks.

"I'm serious! I know you! Something will pop up and you want to get involved! "Don't!", Enzo replies giving Katy a stern look.

"Why don't you contact Marty Jones from probation and maybe psycho analyze some of his parolee's! Use that Forensic Psychology degree to save the world!"

"Ok I will call him." Katy promises.

Enzo still not convinced, says "I heard a rumor you're giving wrestling another go! Please do that! Just don't get into any trouble!"

Katy gives Ray a salute with a smile playing on her lips, "Have fun on your trip. All is well!"

As Ray reluctantly hops into his truck and drives away, he can be heard yelling "Alright! Alright! Alright!"

It's Jenny's debut event. Katy and Jenny are in the dressing room. Katy is giving Jenny a quick pep talk when Sandy and Wendy walk in.

Wendy looks at Jenny and tells her, "Jenny you are taking on Marvelous Mindy! She is tough but beatable! I know you will do great!"

Then she turns to Katy and says "hey Katy! Wanna do me a favor?!"

"Maybe! What is it?!" Katy asks suspiciously.

"Amy Archer sprained her ankle roller skating. They need a replacement to take on Sally Slick! They want me to fill in but I'm not feeling too hot, and Sandy is under contract with that Japanese group and can't compete without their permission!"

Katy pauses, "I'd rather not but if you're not up to it then ok! I will do it!"

Jenny shouts excitedly, "yes! I get to see you in action!"

Wendy tosses Katy a gym bag with Katy's gear, "suit up you're on next!"

Katy lets out a nervous laugh, "I will get you back for this Wendy!"

Katy is now all dressed up and ready to go! As she walks towards the ring, Jenny calls out to her "you're the best Katy! Wipe her out!"

Katy turns around and gives Jenny a thumbs up!

The ring announcer announces, "in this corner we have Sally Slick!"

Sally wearing her signature wet looking purple suit flips off the crowd and they award her with a barrage of boos!

In a booming voice, the ring announcer ignores the crowd, "what a pleasant surprise! Entering the ring after a long sabbatical is the one and only Gorgeous Katy!!"

The crowd goes absolutely nuts rising to their feet and cheering!

The bell rings and the two ladies go right at it! Katy, not missing a beat, hooks Sally's arm and hip tosses her to the mat! Wham! Sally hits hard arching her back in pain! Katy picks her right up and whips her into the ropes! Sally springs off and gets leveled by a dropkick from Katy! The crowd loves it! But Sally Slick is one tough wrestler! She regroups and really takes the fight to Katy! She wants to ruin Katy's return to the ring! She tries to nail Katy with a mule kick but she misses and lands flat on her back! Katy goes to scoop up Sally when she punches Katy right in the gut! Katy staggers back and Sally pops right up grabbing Katy's arm and whips Katy into the ropes! Katy bounces off and ducks a vicious clothes-line from Sally! Katy springs off the opposite ropes and leaps into the air hitting Sally square in the chest with both knees! Sally crashes to the mat with Katy on top! Sally is stunned! Katy hooks her leg as the ref counts 1! 2!! 3!!! Wow!! Katy wins!

The crowd cheers as the ring announcer belts out "in her spectacular return to the ring! The winner of the match is Gorgeous Katy!"

Katy can hear the crowd chant her name: "Katy! Katy! Katy!", as she jogs back to the dressing room! She feels incredible!

Jenny is there waiting and gives Katy a big hug, "that was amazing!"

"Thank you! I was a bit rusty, but it felt great! But now it's your turn! Go get her Jenny! Remember all that you have learned!"

As Jenny slowly makes her way out of the dressing room, she replies "I'm so nervous but yes! I will make you proud!"

Jenny takes deliberate steps to the ring soaking in the whole experience! She hops into the ring and waves to the crowd. She hears the ring announcer say, "in this corner making her pro wrestling debut we have Jet-Set Jenny

Ryan!" To her, it sounds distant. Surreal. The crowd gives her a clap and few people cheer!

"And in this corner is the Marvelous Mindy!" Some in the crowd cheered and some hit her with boos!

The bell rings. Mindy charges straight at Jenny! But Jenny quickly drops to the mat sweeping Mindy's legs out from under her! Mindy slams face first into the mat! Jenny gets behind Mindy putting her foot in an ankle lock! Mindy pounds the mat in frustration! Jenny twists away and Mindy screams in pain. The ref asks Mindy if she wants to submit. Mindy snaps at him, "hell no!" Mindy drags herself across the ring placing her hand on the ropes which forces Jenny to release the hold! The match becomes a back-and-forth battle with both ladies having the advantage then losing it. It's a stalemate until Mindy flies off the ropes hoping to flatten Jenny with a high cross body block! But Jenny catches her midair and uses Mindy's momentum against her! Bam! Jenny slams Mindy on the mat! Mindy is in trouble! Jenny needs to quickly follow up that move with a leg drop or a body slam! But Jenny goes and climbs to the top rope! She waves to the crowd then flies through the air! But no!! Mindy rolls away! Boom! Jenny slams full force into the mat! Whoa! Jenny is gasping for air! Mindy capitalizes on Jenny's mistake by leaping up and crushing Jenny with a knee to the midsection! Mindy covers Jenny for the pin! Jenny tries to kick out, but the ref counts 1! 2!! 3!!! Wow! The ref raises Mindy's hand as the ring announcer proclaims, "the winner of this exciting match is Marvelous Mindy!"

The crowd's reaction is a mix of cheers and boos!

Jenny, a bit dejected, collects herself and slowly walks back to the dressing room, where she is met by Wendy who immediately wants to critique her decision making.

Luckily, Katy steps in and gives Jenny a hug.

"You did great! You can't win them all!"

Jenny looks up at Katy, "I'm so sorry I got too excited, and I screwed up!"

"Forget it! Let's get cleaned up! We are going out to celebrate that you got in there and gave it your all!"

Katy takes Jenny to Izzy's old bar. The place is jumping! Katy immediately sees Donny Franklin! She walks over says "Hello Detective."

He gives her a snarky look, "Hello, Ms. Rachford. But I'm a Lieutenant now"

A lady sitting across from him, looks over and asks Katy, "Ms Rachford?! You're the lady that LT Franklin saved a while ago!"

Katy grins, "oh! Is that what he is telling you? But you can't always believe everything that you hear!"

The lady chuckles and says "ha I knew he was exaggerating! Hi, I'm Detective Tamara Sanders. I'm very pleased to meet you!"

"Oh, thank you! I'm very pleased to meet you too." Katy answers. Then turning to LT Franklin, asks "so? How is business?"

Franklin replies saying "Sorry! No mysterious poisonings just a depressed businessman who took a swan dive off the roof of his building! It's an open and shut case!"

Astonished by Franklin's candor, Katy excuses herself by saying, "oh that's terrible! I feel for his family. But it was nice to meet you Detective Sanders. Do your best to keep him in line!" Detective Sanders laughs as Katy walks away!

Katy finds Jenny sitting down at a table with two beers waiting. Relieved, Katy sits down and takes a beer. She clinks hers against Jenny's saying "cheers to you!" Jenny cracks a half smile and asks, "who are those guys?"

"That's the Detective who was involved in the whole Brenda tragedy. But his new assistant? I've never met her before."

Jenny lets out a sigh, "oh right. So sad."

Katy hits Jenny in the arm lightheartedly, "snap out of it! You did great! I saw you cruising around that ring! The victories will come very quickly!"

The two friends sip their cold beers as a handsome man walks up to the table.

"Hello there! I'm Rob Hamilton. Harriet's son. I couldn't help overhearing you talking to Donny!"

Katy looks up from her half-drunk beer, "oh! You know Franklin?"

"Yeah, from the golf course! Man, he likes to brag! But I heard him say your name. I can't thank you enough for finding my mom's dog! She was driving my daughter and I crazy!"

"Oh, you're very welcome!", Katy quicky adds, "I hope your wife was pleased as well."

"I'm a widower but my daughter and I can now enjoy peace and quiet!"

"Oh, I'm so sorry about your wife."

"It's ok it's been a few years now."

He then looks right into Jenny's eyes and asks Katy "who is this lovely frowning faced lady sitting with you?!"

Katy kicks Jenny under the table. This seems to bring Jenny back from whatever wonderland she escaped to.

"Uh, Hello, I'm Jenny. I'm very happy about your mom's dog!"

Rob smiles, "thank you! I don't know if either of you remember the old bartender who used to work here. But she used to tell this joke."

Rob chuckles and begins, "a horse walks into a bar and the bartender says why the long face? So, Miss Jenny why the long face?!"

Before Jenny can answer, Katy answers "she is ok! She had a minor setback but that's over and done with! Onward and upward! Right Jenny?!"

Jenny looks over at Katy. A look of bewilderment was still on her face "Yes! Onward and upward! Thank you, Rob, for your concern!"

"Of course!" Rob says with a witty smile, "A beautiful face like that should never be wearing a frown!"

It's a nice slow Saturday morning. Katy brings Jenny into her office.

"So, this is where all the mysteries get solved!" Jenny states as she walks around, pretending to inspect the place.

Katy laughingly says "ha! Yeah! That's what I think happens here!"

The girls are chit-chatting as a lady dressed all in black walks in.

"Hello ma'am can I help you?" Katy asks her.

The lady with tears in her eyes, cries "I think my ex-husband was murdered!"

"Oh, I'm so sorry! Please sit down!" Katy says as she gestures to the chair, "do you need me to call the police?!"

The lady in black manages to state in-between weeps, "I've already dealt with them! They aren't interested!'

A bit puzzled, Katy asks "oh! Did you talk with LT. Franklin?!"

"Yes. He wasn't very pleasant to deal with. But let me start over. My name is Carey Lawrence. My ex-husband was Allen Brenner."

Katy puts two and two together, "Was he the businessman who the police say ended his own life?"

"Yes!" Carey cries out! "But I don't believe it! I will provide you with everything I have." She continues to ramble on excitedly, "Although we were divorced, he made me his executor and gave unlimited access to all his business records. I want you to investigate everyone and everything. Even me! I know he didn't kill himself! So, I want you to either prove me wrong or help catch the person responsible!"

Katy pulls out a writing pad and begins to jot down some notes as she asks, "what kind of business was he in? Did he have any employees? Any close friends?! Any lovers? Any enemies?"

"He did financial consulting. He always worked alone. No employees. He also was a very private person. No close friends or lovers that I can think of. But you can check his phone. As for enemies? He was a very nice man. He was just a workaholic! Everyone liked him!", Carey assures her.

"Ok, you've been very helpful. Please leave me all your information and I will consult with Mr Enzo."

Carey gives her information to Katy and walks out the door.

Immediately, Jenny looks at Katy and says "Katy! You must run this by Enzo! Please, please don't start anything without him!"

"Don't worry! I will just review his business dealings and access his computer."

"I know you, Katy! Once you get going you never want to stop! Please be careful! I need you in one piece!"

It's just another inane Monday and Katy is sitting at her desk contem-plat-ing on where to begin. She is still unsure about how she feels about this one. That gut feeling that she usually gets when something is wrong just isn't there. But Katy is a woman who keeps her word and will inves-tigate this to the end regardless of what the outcome will be. There are boxes and boxes filled with all the contents from Allen's office that Carey had delivered. She searches for any signs of depression. She looks for any suicide notes or violent drawings. She can't find a thing! No depression medications or psychiatrist business cards. So, she dives deep into all the business records. She is scouring through Allen's bank accounts for the possibility of any suspicious deposits or withdrawals. She is trying to find out if he was going bankrupt or if someone was extorting money from him. She sees multiple check deposits from Kirov Koffee. "There are a lot of these. I'm going to have to research this company." She says out loud to herself.

Then she gets a text from Jenny: "hey! Are you behaving? Nothing dan-gerous please!"

"Hey, hey! I'm being good. I'm just reviewing banking transactions. But can you look up Kirov Koffee in your system?"

"Hmm." Jenny texts, "I don't want to get in trouble. I will think about it."

"Ok. I understand." Katy writes back. "But please keep it in mind in case their name comes across your desk."

After work Katy and Jenny meet up at the training center.

Wendy runs right up to Jenny, "what did I tell you?! No high risk moves! You had that match won!"

"I know! I know! I've learned my lesson! The hard way!", Jenny answers.

"Alright! Let's move on! But I wanna see how you two vibe as tag team! Suit up! We are having a training tag team match right now! It's you guys' against me and Sadie Shaker!"

"You got it! See ya' in the ring!" Katy yells back to her.

The four ladies are now toe to toe in the center of the ring. Wendy asks, "Katy! Are you ok with Jenny and Sadie kicking things off?!"

"Yeah, that's fine!"

Sadie and Jenny circle then lock up! Sadie puts Jenny in a head lock and drags her over to Wendy's corner tagging her in!

Katy shouts, "Come on! I thought Sadie and Jenny were going to tangle a bit!"

Wendy retorts with a "Jenny needs to learn!"

"Ok! I see how you wanna play!", Katy answers back.

Wendy tears into Jenny and gives her a pounding! Wendy and Sadie keep Jenny on their side of the ring! They tag in and out keeping themselves fresh while Jenny is wiped out!

Katy stamps her feet, "come Jenny! Hang tough! Get over here and tag me in!"

Wendy snap mares Jenny to the mat and applies the sleeper hold! Jenny desperately tries to stretch her fingers and tag in Katy! But she is still inches away! Katy shouts, "reach for me Jenny don't give up!" Then Jenny starts to fade!

Sadie yells "yeah that's it she is done!" Wendy cracks a smile but then suddenly Jenny, using her last bit of energy, lunges forward and taps fingers with Katy!! Wendy is caught completely off guard as Katy slingshots herself over the top rope and nails Wendy with a flying tackle! Wendy hits the mat then rolls away! She hops up and makes the tag to Sadie! But Sadie is greeted by a flying elbow to the nose from Katy! Sadie hits the mat in a daze! Katy lets out a scream and catches a staggering Sadie with a swinging neck breaker! Wham! Sadie is knocked loopy! Katy splashes down on Sadie and slaps the mat counting 1! 2!! 3!!' Katy jumps up and is immediately embraced by Jenny!

Wendy climbs through the ropes saying "we thought we had you Jenny! We really wanted to show you how a good tag team will take advantage of a rookie! But you hung in there and of course Katy was incredible!"

She shakes Katy's hand and says "No hard feelings! We were just making it real!"

Answering Wendy, Katy says "I understand now!". Then, turning to Jenny, she says, "Jenny that was a great lesson!"

As they are changing in the locker room, Jenny approaches Katy.

"I don't think I'm the right partner for you Katy! They had me several times!"

Katy grabs Jenny by the shoulders "nonsense! They put you through the ringer and you shocked them! You're tough as nails with a heart of gold! I wouldn't want to do this with anyone else but you!"

Relieved to hear this, Jenny gives Katy a hug, as Katy bellows, "let's go celebrate!"

Katy is at her desk clicking through Allen's laptop. She is reading his emails and reviewing all his tax returns. But when she clicks on a folder labeled 12J34S it pops up asking for a password. Katy tries all the ones that Carey provided but none of them work!

"That's odd! But Kirov Koffee is really driving me crazy!"

She googles Kirov Koffee and reads that the parent company is based in Moscow.

"Oh! The Russians! This could be something!"

She continues to read that the front man for her area is Dimitri Metroff.

"Hmm I might have to reach out to Eddie Galindo about him!"

She then scrolls through Allen's phone and sees an empty text conversation with the contact name listed as Pie but when she checks the contact page the number is missing. So, she continues to scroll and reads a text from T it says "you lost! Pay up you fool or I will break you!"

Katy, still thinking out loud says to herself, "I wonder if that's that same T who sold drugs at the college?!"

As she contemplates this, Jenny sends a text saying "Kirov Koffee's electric bill is way too high for such a small building! Like 4 times higher than it should be!"

Interesting.

"Great job Jenny! Thank you!" Katy writes back.

Katy's next stop is Eddie Galindo's welding shop. As she approaches, as soon as Eddie sees her, he can't help but cry out, "oh no! Here comes trouble! What's going on now?!"

"Look what I got for you! A full carton of Newport's and a crisp Benjamin Franklin!"

Eddie scoffs, "oh crap! This is gonna be a messy one! Didn't Ray tell you not to come by here? He sure as hell chewed me out about it! But ok! What do you want?!"

"I've got two things to ask you! First is Kirov Koffee and the second is I need to get a hold of T!"

"First off stay away from Kirov Koffee that's Metroff's crew! Hardcore Russian Mobsters! He would sooner kill you than look at you! Second do you need a drug fix? You kids and your Xanax! Yeah, I can hook you up with him!"

"Thank you for T but you're saying Kirov Koffee is dirty?"

"Freaking filthy! Stay the F away from them!"

"Ok I will! But I will go see T soon! Thank you!"

Eddie shakes his head, "Alright but Enzo never needs to know about this, ok?!"

Katy nods in response, "ok!"

Katy is finally home sitting on the couch with a glass of wine.

Jenny comes home and jokes, "hey I'm glad to see our lights are still on! Boy! So many people neglect their electric bills!"

Katy excitedly looks up, "Come sit down I have lots to tell you!"

"Ok! I will grab a glass and you can pour me some wine and fill me in."

Katy pours the wine. "Allen has a ton of deposits from that company Kirov Koffee that I was asking you about! They are Russian mobsters! Then he had a threatening text from T! He is a drug dealer who sells to the students at Gunness University and apparently now he is also a sports gambling bookie!"

Jenny's mouth drops. "Are you crazy?! Hand all that over to the police! Let them question those people!"

"They already closed the case! They won't bother with some questionable bank deposits or a single text that can be interpreted in many ways. I will have to give them something concrete!" "This could get very dangerous! I really think you should wait for Enzo to get back, Katy! You are at a good place now to hit the pause button."

Just as Jenny finishes her sentence, Katy's phone rings! It's Brett Rodgers, the owner of the wrestling group that Katy first started out with.

Brett shouts through the phone, "Katy!!!!!! How ya doing?! I heard you're back in the wrestling game!! Why didn't you call me?!"

"My friend Jenny convinced me to give it another shot! I was thinking about contacting you, but Hannah is your big star!"

"Nonsense! Our Instagram page is loaded with messages from people clamoring for your return! How about another match with Hannah?!"

"Oh wow! Thank you! But I'm concentrating now on tag team wrestling with my girl Jenny!" "You're in luck! Savannah and Hannah Glamour are now a tag team! I know you would love to get some payback on them!"

"You know I would! But I wouldn't want to disrespect Mr. King!"

Brett understands but continues with, "well today is your lucky day! I've already spoken with him and we made a deal! He says if you want to go get the Glamour Sisters, he is behind you one hundred percent! Plus, Shannon Star is super afraid of you! So, she really convinced Kevin to let you go!"

Katy is pleasantly surprised by this news. "Wow! Ok!", she tells Brett over the phone.

"Stop by the lumberyard when you have time, and we will hash out all the details!" Brett tells Katy.

"Thank you, Brett! I will be in touch!" Katy hangs up the phone.

Jenny stares at Katy, "OMG! The Glamour Sisters? I'm not ready for them!"

"We will be! Jenny, I can promise you that!"

The next day, Jenny leaves for work, she says to Katy "I'm off! Have a great day! But please don't do anything else but office work on that case!"

"You got it! I'm just gonna review some paperwork! Don't you worry!"

Katy starts flipping through some contracts and more emails hoping to find something to corroborate Carey's gut feeling. She then looks at her watch and says "oh! It's noon! T will be leaving the quad soon. I'd better head on over there!"

Katy arrives just as T is leaving. She stops him, "hey are you T?"

He looks her up and down then says "ya! Maybe! What cha looking for?!"

"I want to ask you a few questions!"

"What?! You ain't no cop!"

"No! No, I'm not! But a very nice lady wants to know what happened to her ex-husband?"

"Who?"

"Allen Brenner!"

"Oh man! Poor Al why the heck would he do that?"

"Do you know what happened to him?"

"Yeah! He jumped off a roof!"

"You didn't push him? You wrote him a nasty text!"

T stops Katy with a hand gesture, and looks her dead in the eye, "yo! Hold up! Me and Al were boys! He was one of my best customers! That text was a love chat! I bust his balls every time he loses! Which isn't very often! Plus, it was only five hundred dollars! I'm not doing 20 years in prison for five hundred dollars! So, unless you want some Xanax. Then I'm gonna go!" T jogs off and hops in a car and drives away!

Katy, left alone, says to herself, "he seemed truthful! So, I guess I'm gonna have to check out Kirov Koffee one of these days!"

Next stop, Rodgers' lumberyard where Katy is greeted by Brett with open arms!

"Katy my dear! Let's talk in my office."

They sit down.

"Katy, you look great! How ya been? I'm so glad that you're back in the

game! So, who is this Jenny friend of yours? I heard she got beat by Marvelous Mindy! Are you sure that you want her for a partner?!"

Cooly, Katy says "thank you I've been busy. Jenny is still learning but she gives it her all. Plus, she is a very loyal friend!"

"Ok but I will have to see her in action. I will set up a match with you two taking on Busybody Brittany George and Crystal Martin!" But if Jenny loses it for your team, then I want you to really consider going back to being a singles competitor."

"We won't lose! But that's fair! If that happens, I will definitely consider that!"

"Great! It hasn't been the same around here without you! This place comes alive when you're here! By the way how is Izzy doing?"

"Izzy is taking Canada by storm! She is amazing! I really miss her!"

"Me too!"

Then in walks Hannah and with a scowl on her face. "Oh! Look what the cat dragged in? This is my promotion! Don't even think about coming for me again!"

Brett snaps at Hannah, "hey! You be quiet! Katy is loved around here! If you're afraid of her then that's on you!"

Hannah just laughs and walks away!

"Wow! She is still as friendly as a rattlesnake!" Katy says once she is just out of earshot.

Brett laughs and says, "that's for sure!"

Back at the apartment Jenny has been anxiously waiting for Katy's return.

"Where have you been? What were you doing? I was worried sick! "

"I'm ok I just went to the school and asked T a few questions."

"Please never go ask anyone involved in this mess any questions by yourself! Promise me that!" "Ok you're right! I shouldn't do that. But I did stop by and talked to Brett! He wants to set up a tag team match to see how we do before we go after the Glamour sisters!"

"Oh wow! Who are we facing?"

"Busybody Brittany and Crystal Martin!"

"Are they any good?!"

"They are good enough! But we will be ready!"

"Yes! I'm gonna train like crazy!" Jenny says, as Katy gives her a hug.

"Me too! Now what's for dinner?"

"Chicken or fish?" Jenny answers

"I will flip you for it!"

Jenny goes to take a coin out of her pocket when Katy scoops her up and tosses her on the couch!

"I win!" Katy jokes.

Jenny rolls around on the couch laughing "you got me this time!"

Katy is racking her brain with this case. She is trying so hard to figure out if Allen was murdered or just took his own life. She keeps staring at Allen's laptop screensaver. It has the words "What's the opposite of progress? "Constantly bouncing around the screen.

"Ugh! That's it!" Katy exclaims with frustration. 'I gotta go check out Kirov Koffee! But I will wait for Jenny!"

She goes for a run to clear her head! She comes home, takes a shower and watches some old videos of Hannah Glamour's greatest matches while she prepares dinner. When Jenny arrives home, Katy proudly tells her " I made your favorite dish Pan Seared Salmon and asparagus!

Mmm good!" Jenny says "thank you! But what's the catch?!"

"Relax! Enjoy your food then we will talk."

Jenny finishes eating, "that was magnificent. Now what are you scheming?"

"Nothing dangerous. Let's just take a quick drive."

Jenny rolls her eyes and reluctantly agrees. They arrive in front of the Kirov Koffee building and Jenny says "whoa! Why are we here? I thought you said this place is run by the Russian mob?!"

"Relax! I'm just going to take a quick look around! I will be right back! Just keep the car the running!"

As Katy walks away, Jenny yells after her "please be careful!"

Katy sneaks up to the side of the building. She can hear lots of machinery running. She also hears a bunch of men speaking in Russian. She hops up on a box to peek in the window when everything goes black!

As she regains consciousness, she can hear men talking in Russian. Then as her eyes adjust, she can see that she is seated in front of a well-dressed Russian man who is smoking a Cuban cigar. In a heavy Russian accent, he asks "How can I help you?"

Groggily, Katy asks "are you Dimitri Metroff?! Did you have Allen Brenner killed?!"

The man scoffs "are you trying to interrogate me?! Are you serious? Am I being...umm? What do you Americans call it? Am I being punked?! Did Sergei put you up to this?!"

"I don't know anyone named Sergei! I'm just here to get some answers for Allen Brenner's family! They are paying me so they can have some sort of closure! What's your business relationship with Allen? What are you really manufacturing here?!"

Dimitri guffaws "Viktor! Check out the balls on this one! She thinks she is KGB!"

A mean looking thug replies, "want me to put a bullet in her head?!"

Dimitri answers back mockingly "not yet! This is some good entertainment! Listen Miss America! I'm a businessman I don't discuss my business with strangers! As for Brenner, we had a good thing going! I don't get rid of good things! But you should know that back in my country if someone wants somebody gone they do it very loudly! They don't make it look like an accident or suicide. They cut off certain body parts and stuff them in people's mouths! They want everyone to know that they did it! But me being a noble businessman I abhor such things!" Casually, as he then checks his phone, Dimitri carries on, "Miss America! Who is the sweetie in the car? My associate is keeping an eye on her!"

Katy, now very concerned, "That's my friend! She just drove me here! She knows nothing!" "Ok! Now what am I supposed to do with you?", Dimitri snaps as Viktor gets behind Katy and places a gun to the side of her head!

Dimitri looks at Katy with impressed amusement, "Wow! You don't flinch! Hey Viktor! Give her a swift kick in the ass and throw her out the door! And as for you, Miss America! Don't ever come back here!"

And with one swift move, the mean looking thug Viktor picks Katy straight up and gives her an actual kick in the butt! He then throws her up in the air and out the door! Katy lands with a thud! But she gets right up and dusts herself off! As she walks back to the car, she can see her hands trembling!

"Boy! That was stupid", she whispers to herself.

When she gets to the car, she can see Jenny is a nervous wreck!

Jenny quickly smacks Katy in the arm! "Where the hell have you been?! I was losing my mind! I kept thinking I saw a red dot on my chest!"

"I'm so sorry! What I did was foolish! Thank you for being here! But I'm pretty sure that

those guys didn't kill Allen!"

Katy takes a much-needed break from the case and focuses completely on getting Jenny and herself ready for their tag team match! They bounce around the ring trading holds and develop some new strategies! Jenny works on her flying leap from the top rope! Finally, Katy says "we are ready!" They arrive at the arena and get dressed for action.

Jenny says "Thank you Katy! I feel great! I have a good feeling about this!"

Katy puts her hand on Jenny's shoulder, "just be wise and give it your all! We can beat those two!"

When they get to the ring, Busybody Brittany George and Crystal Martin are already in their corner and they can hear the ring announcer say "now entering the ring is Jet-Set Jenny Ryan and Gorgeous Katy! They are team Elegance!" The crowd erupts with applause! Katy and Brittany open the match with a blistering barrage of tomahawk chops! They go shot for shot with neither one wanting to give any ground! Finally, Katy ducks a blow from Brittany! Her momentum makes her spin around! Katy immediately grabs her from behind and lifts Brittany into the air! Bam! Brittany's butt slams into Katy's knee sending a shockwave up and down Brittany's spine! She hops around the ring holding her backside! Katy follows up by leveling her with a clothesline! Brittany lays on the mat in a daze! So, Katy quickly runs and tags in Jenny! She sails over the ropes and hits Brittany with a leg drop! The crowd cheers! Jenny yanks Brittany off the mat and whips her into the ropes! Brittany bounces off and gets hit with a flying elbow! Wow! Jenny crashes down on Brittany and goes for the pin! The ref counts 1! When Crystal comes swooping in and kicks poor Jenny right upside the head stopping the three count! Crystal quickly drags Brittany to her corner and makes the tag! Katy is screaming at the referee but to no avail! Now Crystal jumps down and starts choking Jenny! The ref screams at Crystal to stop or she will be disqualified! The match goes on and Jenny takes a beating! But just when you think all is lost, she dives out of the way of a giant splash and Brittany slams face first into the corner turnbuckles! Jenny manages to stagger over and make the tag to Katy! The crowd goes wild as Katy hits Brittany with a mule kick! Then Katy picks her up and gives Brittany a DDT! Wow! Brittany's head slams full force into the mat! Brittany is seeing stars! Katy pounces on her for the pin as Crystal comes running in for the save! But Jenny musters up enough strength to hit Crystal with a shoulder tackle! There is no escape for Brittany as the ref counts 1! 2!! 3!!! They did it! Team Elegance wins!!! The crowd loves it! Jenny is absolutely elated! She swings Katy around in a bear hug, screaming, "We did it! We actually did it! Drinks are on me!"

Later at the bar, Katy and Jenny are toasting to their victory when Detective Sanders walks up. "Damn Katy! I heard Franklin say that you wrestled or something. But I didn't believe him! So when I saw you in the ring tonight I was like, wow! You got some moves girl!"

Katy laughs. "Thank you! It was so great to get a win!"

Sanders, now more serious, responds, "Hey! I caught wind that you were snooping around asking about Allen Brenner. I won't say anything, but don't let Franklin find out! That lazy sack hates to do any actual work!"

"Ok. Thanks for the tip!"

With that, Jenny waves bye to Detective Sanders and tells Katy, "Katy, you don't know how happy I feel! That was so great!"

Katy nods in agreement. "oh, believe me I know!"

Suddenly Rob Hamilton comes sneaking up behind Jenny, "wow! I hear you two are wrestling superstars!"

Jenny cracks a huge smile in response, "Katy is! She is the best!"

"Nonsense! I'm sure my Jenny is amazing as well!"

Katy begins to drift back to thinking about the Brenner case as Rob and Jenny flirtatiously banter.

"What's the opposite of progress?" Katy mutters under her breath,

"What?", Rob asks.

"Oh nothing!"

"No tell me!"

"Ok! What's the opposite of progress?!"

Rob laughs, "that's an old political joke! The opposite of progress is Congress!"

Katy's eyes open wide. "Is that eight letters long?"

"Yeah!", Rob laughs.

Katy gasps, "OMG! That's probably the password!"

Now, it's Jenny's turn to pipe in, "for that laptop file?"

"I hope so!" Katy says excitedly.

"Are you guys still on the Brenner thing?!", Rob asks. "I'm shocked that the cops didn't talk to my mom's friend Henry Davis from the kennel club! His apartment window overlooks the building were Brenner jumped off!"

"that building wouldn't happen to have any cameras would it?" Katy asks.

"Not that high up! But my mom's crazy friend does! He has one watching the fire escape, so nobody tries to break in!"

Upon hearing this wonderful piece of information, Katy gives Rob a big bear hug "I bet it has a perfect view of the roof! Thank you, Rob! This might be the big break that I was hoping for!"

Later that night, Katy fires up Allen's laptop! She immediately tries Congress, but that's not it! So she tries congress. Again nothing! She lets out a scream "crap! This sucks!" Then she thinks! "Allen is a financial guy! Let me try Congr3ss." Bam!! That's it! The file opens! Katy begins to read it.

"Are you freaking kidding me?! Boy did we get played!"

She is reading a whole series of text messages between Allen Brenner and Jill Silverman! It seems that they have been having an affair! But Allen is furious because Jill lied saying that she was already divorced! Jill tried to salvage the relationship by hiring Enzo and Katy to get dirt on her husband! She tried telling Allen she spent all this money to prove that her husband was a lying cheater and that her relationship with Allen was justified! But Allen was not having any of that! He said flat out that she was a lying manipulative bitch and that he couldn't believe that he had ever called her his Sweetie Pie! Then Jill got nasty and threatened to kill Allen if he tried to break up with her!

"Wow!" Katy thinks out loud. "That's why he made this file! He must have really been afraid that she would do something to him and that she would be able to ditch his phone!"

Katy slams the laptop shut. "I gotta head right over to Mr. Davis's apartment!"

When Katy arrives, Mr. Davis is hesitant to open the door.

"Go away.", he tells Katy. "I'm not showing you my camera!"

"Please sir I'm Katy Rachford! I found Harriet Hamilton's dog!"

Henry swings the door wide open, "well, any friend of Harriet is a friend of mine!"

"Did someone come by asking about your camera?"

"Yes! Some fancy pants rich lady! She wanted to see it because she said someone stole her Mercedes recently! I was a little suspicious, so I told her my computer was going haywire and to come back in the morning."

"That was a very wise move! So, can I review some of the footage?"

"Yes! Of course!"

Katy clicks through and Bam! There it is! Jill Silverman leading Mr. Brenner to the roof's edge at gun point! You can see Allen pleading with her! You can see Allen giving her his phone! Then it looks like things began to calm down! Then suddenly Jill shoves Allen off the side of the roof to his doom! Katy quickly makes a thumb drive file of the video. She is about to walk away but thinks better of it. "I'd better email this part to myself just in case!"

Henry asks, "was that helpful?!"

"Absolutely." Katy says. "But if anyone comes back looking for it immediately call the police!"

Henry replies "you got it missy!"

Katy goes to leave the building, wham! Everything goes black!

Katy comes to but she is tied to a chair!

Jill Silverman walks over to her, "hand it over!"

"I don't know what you're talking about!"

Jill leans in. Katy can feel her breath on her face.

"Give me the God Damn video!", Jill demands as she rummages through Katy's pockets.

To Katy's chagrin, Jill finds it! She immediately drops it to the floor and crushes it with a stomp of her foot.

Defiantly, Katy tells her, "That's not gonna work!"

Jill interrupts, "Oh Mr. Davis! He is about to have an unfortunate accident! Faulty stove! So sad!"

A younger man walks in and nervously looks to Jill, "now what do we do? You said this would be easy!"

Jill snaps back, "shut up! We need to think of a way to get rid of her!"

The doorbell rings! The younger man goes to the door and peaks through the peephole. There is a guy with his hat pulled down low holding a pizza.

"Honey, a pizza guy is here!"

Irritated, Jill says "stupid idiots! It's for across the street! Send him there!"

As the younger man goes to open the door he is knocked to the floor! The pizza guy takes off his hat and dumps the pizza on the guy! It's Ray Enzo! He knocks the guy out with a Black Jack

then points his gun at Jill! But Jill has a knife held against Katy's throat!

"One false move and I slit her throat!"

"Relax," Enzo tells Jill, "We can make a deal here! If you let her go, I will let you go!"

Boom!! The back door gets smashed in!

Jill turns around to look and gets pistol whipped by Ray! She drops the knife and collapses to the floor!

It's Detective Sanders! She runs and handcuffs both Jill and the strange man! Enzo's face turns as red as a tomato! "Katy!!! I wanna strangle you! What did I say? I said don't get involved in Anything!! But no, you had to question a drug dealing sports bookie! Then you tried to spy on and interrogate Dimitri Metroff!! If he had even the slightest inkling that you knew anything about what he does, he would have you chopped up into dog food! You'd be getting crapped out right now from Chester's ass!"

Tamara turns to Ray "calm down!", But then she lays into Katy! "Girl! You're a fool! The second you got the password you should have called me! I'm not Franklin! I care!"

Katy with tears in her eyes apologizes to the both of them, "I'm so sorry! I just can't not help someone when they ask! I get fixated on finding the truth! I just wanna help people!"

Tamara unties Katy and she braces herself for whatever Ray is about to throw at her! But Ray snatches her up in a big bear hug! He gives her a peck on the forehead, "oh Katy! You just took ten years off of my life! I couldn't live with myself if anything was to happen to you! You're so amazing! But a huge pain in my ass!"

Back at the apartment the next morning Jenny can clearly see that Katy has been put through the ringer! She gives her a hug, "you must definitely have a guardian angel watching over you!"

Katy laughs, "Jenny! I'm pretty sure I do! Well, you better take a seat for what I'm about to show you! It's the morning paper and the front cover says, "Lieutenant Donny Franklin yet again saves our community!" Katy pauses and pretends to puke, "that weasel just took credit for our hard work! He is quoted as saying "I had my suspicions all along!"

"What a crock! Carey Lawrence knows the truth! So do Detective Sanders, Ray and of course me! We all know you made this happen! I'm so freaking proud of you!"

Katy smiles and says "thank you Jenny! You've been my friend for a long time! I'm so happy you came here!"

Jenny says "alright! Let's have some mindless fun today! But tomorrow we prepare for battle!" They invite Rob and Ray out to the indoor arcade and go cart track! They spend the day shooting aliens and crashing around the track! They end the day with a toast! "To all those that we have loved and lost!"

The next morning, at 6am, Katy is all dressed up and ready to go. She goes to Jenny's room to wake her up, but Jenny is already dressed and is talking to herself in the mirror, "you've been through so much this year! You want this! You deserve this now go get it!"

Katy replies to Jenny's mirror image "wow! With that spirit nothing will stop us!"

It's time for Katy and Jenny to shine! No team has worked harder than them! They sit in the dressing room practicing positive energy breathing when a lady hands them a note:

"We love you girls!
You're winners in our eyes no matter what!
But we want you to give them hell tonight!"

Ray, Rob and Tamara!

Katy folds it nicely and tucks it away as she turns towards Jenny, "the Glamour sisters go home defeated tonight!"

"Absolutely!" Jenny gleefully replies.

They get the signal and start to make their way to the ring! As soon as the crowd sees them it's like an explosion! The whole building is shaking! As they enter the ring the announcer says "Ladies and Gentlemen! This is the main event of the evening! It's a special lady's tag team match scheduled for 2 out of 3 falls!"

Confused, Katy asks the ref "so when did this happen?"

The ref tells her that "Hannah really pushed for it just in case you got lucky! 2 out 3 is better for her team!"

Katy just shakes her head! She can hear the announcer speaking, "in this corner is Gorgeous Katy and Jet-Set Jenny Ryan! Together they are Team Elegance!" The crowd goes wild! "But in this corner are two ladies that are known all over the world! Let's hear it for Hannah and Savannah! The Glamour Sisters!"

They get a few whistles but mostly boos!

Hannah signals to the crowd to kiss her butt!

It's the confrontation that everyone has been waiting for! Katy and Hannah start the match off with a bang! Hannah charges at Katy like a woman possessed! Katy simply sidesteps Hannah's charge, sending Hannah crashing into the ropes! Katy flies up behind Hannah and catches her with a knee to the back! Hannah drops to the mat like a sack of wheat! But Hannah is tough as nails and goes on offense! She tosses Katy around the ring and ties her up in knots! Hannah has Katy trapped in a Boston Crab! Katy's face grimaces in pain! The ref asks if she wants to submit! But Katy shouts "no!" Then in one swift motion Katy spins her body around and breaks the hold! Hannah goes to jump on Katy but gets nailed with a boot to the chest! Hannah flies backwards and crashes to the mat! Katy picks up Hannah and hits her with a German suplex! Wow! Everyone heard that thud! The back of Hannah's head slammed right into the mat! Hannah's eyes roll to the back of her head! Savannah is in shock! Katy leaps up and hits Hannah with a giant splash! Katy hooks Hannah's leg as the ref counts 1! 2!! 3!!! What?! Did that just happen? Katy pins Hannah for the first fall! The ref raises Katy's hand as the ring announcer says, "the winners of the first fall is Team Elegance!!"

The crowd is in a state of complete joy! Katy goes and hugs Jenny! They are elated! Hannah is furious! The rules state they must start the next fall! Katy goes to lock up with Hannah and she gives Katy a shove! She runs to go tag in Savannah but Katy grabs her from behind! Katy whips Hannah into the ropes! She flies off and Katy nails her with a clothesline! Katy runs to spring off the ropes but Savannah and their friend Rebecca Rage yank Jenny off of the ring apron! They are pummeling her! They slam Jenny face first into the ring post then start to stomp the life out of her! Katy dives out of the ring to save Jenny! She yanks Savannah off but gets hit with a steel chair from Rebecca! OMG! Katy is out cold! Hannah from inside the ring screams "throw her back in!" So, Rebecca tosses a barely conscious Katy back in the ring! Hannah pounces on top of her! The ref counts 1! 2!! 3!!!

"Boo!!"

The Glamour sisters win the second fall! The crowd is livid as the ring announcer says "the winners of the second fall are the Glamour sisters!"

Jenny runs in the ring and cradles Katy! The ref tells her "Hey! If she can't continue, then your team will forfeit!"

Jenny holds Katy and whispers to her "don't worry they cheated! You're too hurt to compete!" Just then Katy's eyes open and she says, "I can do it but be ready to come in!"

Katy courageously staggers to her feet! Hannah yells "it's over I will finish her right now!" The crowd boos! Hannah and Katy lock up! Hannah tries to yank Katy's hair! But Katy hits Hannah with a forearm smash to the nose! Incredible! How was Katy able to do that?!

Hannah staggers back! Katy stumbles and falls but makes the tag to Jenny! The crowd is reenergized as Jenny comes in like a tornado! She drop kicks Hannah right into her corner! She then yanks Savannah over the ropes and slams her into the mat! Savannah pops right up but gets leveled by a clothesline! Jenny leaps up and nails Savannah with a knee to the forehead! Savannah is in trouble! Jenny runs to spring off the ropes but Hannah yanks Jenny's hair from behind! Jenny falls to the mat but pops right back up and spins right around giving Hannah an elbow to the jaw! Wow! Hannah falls off the ring apron! So, Savannah tries to blindside Jenny but Jenny sees her coming! She catches Savannah midair and power slams Savannah to the mat!! Jenny follows right up with a leg drop! She then runs and climbs to the top rope! But Hannah and Rebecca run around to yank her off! Katy somehow has enough strength left to tackle Hannah, but it looks like Rebecca will get her! Then from out of the crowd comes Wendy Wakeford and she nails Rebecca with a knee to the gut! It's pandemonium on the outside of the ring! Jenny, unfazed, leaps into the air! A hush falls over the crowd as Jenny nails Savannah with the giant splash! Hannah desperately tries to get into the ring, but Katy holds her back! Everyone counts along as the referee hits the mat for 1! 2!!   3 ! ! ! History has just been made right before your very eyes! Katy rolls into the ring and is picked up by Jenny! They embrace as the referee raises their hands and the ring announcer shouts "what you all just witnessed here was incredible! The winners of the third fall and the match are Gorgeous Kay and Jet-Set Jenny Ryan Team Elegance!! "

The crowd shouts "Katy! Jenny! Katy! Jenny!"

Back in the dressing room Jenny and Katy are still in shock! Jenny feels the welt on the back of Katy's head!

"You must be in so much pain! I'm in awe on how you came through!"

"We've been through too much together over the years! I had to overcome it! But I'm probably going to get an X-ray!"

Just then Ray and Rob along with Tamara come running in! They can't stop talking about how awesome that was!

Tamara asks Ray "so they won the big match! What's next for Katy's investigative future?!" Ray replies "well first off, I'm taking Katy to the hospital! Then when she has recovered, I'm letting her relax at my buddy's resort in Cozumel Mexico! I know nothing will happen there!" Katy does another fourth wall break and smiles! "The Gipsy Kings Volare" begins to play!!

KATY IN COZUMEL.

Katy lays on an extremely comfortable lounge chair as she soaks up the sun and gazes into the clear blue sea. She sips on a pina colada, "Wow! I really needed this! It's my very own Cozumel vacation! A chance to relax and escape all the drama as of late!"

She looks around and sees a young couple holding hands and laughing, "Is this your honeymoon?"

The lady replies "no. It's our first wedding anniversary!"

"Oh, that's wonderful! Congratulations!" Then she goes back to her pina colada and skims through her Kindle reading a short story. It's about this retired Detective who claims to have saved the President from a reckless driver and all his misadventures in the army reserves. She laughs as he talks about setting Fort Dix on fire and how he fell in love with Caroline Roberts the Commanding General of the base!

"Ha! I bet he did! But I'm sure she didn't give him the time of day!"

After an enjoyable day in the sun, she heads back to her room and stops by the front desk. Carmen is behind the counter. "Hola, Miss Katy! I hope everything is to your liking?! Mr. Mendoza told us to take very good care of you!"

"Oh yes! Thank you!"

Then Carmen says, "a bunch of people are taking the shuttle bus over to the Casino later, do you want to go?"

Katy politely says "no thank you. I've had enough adventures lately. I'm going to stay at the resort. But I will be hitting up the Hibachi grill later!"

Carmen replies, "mmm! Excellent choice!"

Katy goes up to her room for a shower. She gets all dressed up for dinner. She stops by the lobby bar and has a martini.

There she meets two brothers, Brian and Bradley Young from Sioux City Iowa.

Brian asks Katy "hey! Where are all the single chicks at?"

Bradley interrupts saying, "please ignore him!"

Katy laughs, "I know a bunch of people are going to the Casino. Maybe you will get lucky?!" Brian replies, "yeah?! Well alright!"

The two brothers run off and Katy goes to the Hibachi grill.

She is dazzled by the Chef's skill as he flips his utensils around and makes huge flames with the alcohol! He pops shrimp and veggies into her mouth while making an onion volcano! She has a wonderful time.

Back in her room she puts on Romancing the Stone and nods off.

She is awakened by the sound of a lady screaming and crying. Katy peeks out her door and sees the lady from the beach from earlier that day.

"Are you ok? What happened?", Katy asks her.

The lady is in tears, "my husband was kidnapped!"

"What?! Come to my room. We will figure this all out."

Katy hands the lady a bottle of water to calm her down and then the lady starts to speak.

"My name is Linda Wagner and my husband's name is Anthony. We are from Stamford, CT."

"Ok Linda what happened? Why would anyone want to kidnap your husband?"

Linda replies, "We were on the bus coming back from the Casino when a van cut us off. Then the next thing I know a group of masked men with guns stormed in and took my husband. These two guys tried to help but the men shoved guns in their faces! They just beat Anthony and dragged him away!"

Katy, with a concerned look on her face asks, "what did the police say?!"

"They said it sometimes happens down here and they usually just want money. The police said that they will keep me informed."

Katy gives her a hug, "ok, you're staying with me tonight. Then tomorrow we will come up with a plan. I've done some investigative work, so I have a pretty good idea on how to start."

The next morning Katy comes into the room with a plate of pancakes and two glasses of fresh squeezed orange juice.

"Good morning, Linda. You need to eat something. Then we will work through this." Katy declares in her most cheerful voice.

Linda takes a few bites and drinks the juice, "I can't believe what happened! I was hoping it was a just bad dream."

"It's awful! But now we will get you some answers! First, let's go to the front desk. I want to know everything about the bus driver and that Casino."

They arrive at the front desk and see Carmen walking with a crutch and her left ankle all wrapped up!

"Whoa! What happened to you? You weren't on the shuttle bus last night, were you?!"

Carmen responds "no, I wasn't there. But that whole incident was awful! I hurt myself at my second job. But enough about that. How can I help you?!"

"Well, I hope you heal up quick! But I was hoping that you could get me the name of the bus driver from last night and also what can you tell me about the Casino?" Katy says.

"Juan Garcia? He is a good man but sure you can talk to him. As for the Casino? A bunch of the hotels and resorts around here use it so I don't think they would want to jeopardize their business by being involved in a tourist kidnapping. But I know it's owned by a corporation called Mexibest. They own many types of businesses here in Mexico."

"Thank you, Carmen. Now please go sit down and rest that ankle!"

As Linda and Katy walk away from Carmen, Linda whispers to Katy "so what do you think? Do you think the bus driver, or the Casino may be involved?!"

"I don't think so but I'm not taking any chances! Better to check out everything."

Linda stops Katy and says "I don't even know you, but I feel so comfortable with you! Why are you helping a stranger?!"

Katy replies with "I had a good friend who would always quote John Lewis and he would say "if not us, then who? If not now, then when?" To me that means if you see someone in need then it's your obligation to help!"

Linda pats Katy on the shoulder "they don't make them like you anymore! This is a terrible situation but I'm so lucky to have met you!"

"Let's save that luck for when you get your husband back. But now let's go talk to Juan."

They catch Juan as he is coming into work. Katy walks up and says "hello Juan, I'm Katy and this is Linda. Her husband was the one abducted last night."

"Santa Maria!" Juan gasps, "I'm so sorry! They just cut me off and stormed the bus!"

"Did anyone approach you asking who was on the bus or what time it was leaving?" Katy asks.

"No, but the schedule is posted inside of the Casino, so anyone would be able to find that out." Katy thanks Juan but then asks, "is there anything that you think might help us? Something one of the abductors might have said or some identifiable features. Like a tattoo or maybe a limp?!" Juan replies, "I did tell the police that one of the men only had four fingers on his left hand. No pinkie!"

Katy thanks Juan again for talking to her. Then she and Linda walk away.

Linda immediately whispers to Katy, "do you think he is involved?"

"No." Katy replies, "He wasn't nervous and genuinely seemed concerned."

Katy takes Linda to the lobby bar and says "ok! I want to know everything! The good, the bad, and the ugly before we talk with the police and go poking around the Casino! Who are you guys? Are you rich? Are you involved in any criminal activity? Do either of you have any enemies? Tell me everything! Don't leave anything out!"

Linda says, "we are from Stamford Connecticut. I give private piano lessons to kids in Greenwich. My husband works in NYC for a small advertising firm. We don't do anything illegal! I know his father does some accounting work for some hedge funds on Wall Street but that's quite boring. We give to charity, and we keep to ourselves."

Katy follows up by saying "is this your first marriage? Is it also his? No jilted lovers?!"

Linda says "yes! This is the first marriage for both of us! No crazy ex-lovers!"

Katy, in a calming voice explains, "ok, ok, I just need to know. Because what you think isn't really important sometimes turns out to be a major problem!" Then she asks Linda for the business card that the police gave her. Katy reads it aloud: "Captain Hector Lopez 013-555-7690." She calls but the call goes immediately to voicemail. Katy leaves a message: "hello Captain Lopez. My name is Katy and I'm here with Linda Wagner. Please give us a call back as soon as you can!"

Linda tears up, "this is awful! I hope they are trying to find Anthony!"

"Let's not have any negativity! I want you to go lay down. But if you hear anything please let me know ASAP!"

Linda agrees and goes back to her room.

Meanwhile Katy goes to the front desk and starts to talk to Carmen.

"Some vacation! I came here to get away from drama! Not to be waist deep in it!"

Carmen replies, "I feel so bad for her. But as for you? I don't think I ever met anyone who would be helpful to a complete stranger!"

Then Carmen sighs and sits down in a chair and rubs her ankle.

Katy politely asks, "please tell me how that happened?"

"No, no. I don't think you'd understand!"

"Try me! I've seen and heard it all!"

"Ok, but please don't think poorly of me. My family needs the money!"

"Of course not! I'd never do that!"

Carmen musters up the courage and says, "have you ever heard of Lucha Libre?!"

Katy pauses for a second and says "yes! That's Mexican Pro Wrestling!"

Carmen, being a bit surprised, says "yes! Wow! I didn't think you would know that!"

Katy laughs, "I actually have a fair amount of experience in that subject!"

"What? You like to watch it?!"

Katy replies, "go to YouTube and search Gorgeous Katy vs Hannah Glamour!"

Carmen searches YouTube and begins to watch.

"Incredible you're a wrestler and you beat Hannah Glamour! She is famous!"

Katy humbly says, "yes I did!"

Carmen takes Katy's hand, "May I ask you for an extremely important favor?"

"Umm, ok."

"I think it's Devine intervention that you're here. First to help Linda but also to hopefully help me. Can you fill in for me tonight?! I'm supposed to have a match, but I can't wrestle like this and if I don't show up, I forfeit and lose the money that my family needs." Carmen explains.

"I would but I'm not you! We don't look at all alike!"

Carmen laughs, "no, no! I'm a masked wrestler! I'm Princesa Rosada! The Pink Princess! You'd be perfect!"

Katy shakes her head. "What a vacation! First, I'm helping with a kidnapping and now I'm gonna be back in the ring wrestling!"

Katy is sitting by the pool when Linda runs up.

Excitedly, Linda tells Katy, "I got a call from the Police Captain. Do you want to go with me to talk with him?"

"Yes! Absolutely!"

Carmen hooks them up with a taxi and they go to the Police Headquarters. When they arrive they are greeted by Captain Lopez who takes them into his office. Katy immediately starts to pepper him with questions.

"Why haven't you found him yet? Who did this? What are their demands? Why did this happen? Who is the man with a missing finger?"

Captain Lopez takes his time then says "despacio! I'm sorry I mean slow down. One question at a time. First off, I have some of my best people on this. We definitely don't want tourists abducted. There are a lot of different groups that do this. I know we will be hearing something very soon. As for the man with the missing finger? Lots of drug cartels do that as a punishment when someone makes a mistake. I'm also in the process of obtaining video footage from the Casino to see if anyone was following Mr. Wagner. I understand how upsetting this is, but when it comes to an abducted tourist it's usually all about getting money. So, I can say with some certainty that your husband will be back with you, and all will be well."

Linda just sits there sobbing as Katy says "ok. I'm glad you're working on this, but I think we should also go to the US Embassy and see what the US. State Department can do."

Captain Lopez reluctantly agrees, "ok, but they are usually more of a hassle than a help."

Katy calls the Embassy, and they inform her that she and Linda can come by tomorrow. She thanks Captain Lopez and they leave.

As they walk out Katy consoles Linda, "I have a good feeling about Captain Lopez. I originally thought he would be useless and uncaring, but I was wrong. I think he will help you. Now let's get back to the resort."

They arrive back at the resort and Katy sees Carmen, "do you have everything for me?"

Carmen says "oh yes! When you get there ask for Matilda."

"Ok great! I will make you proud! But now I need you to take good care of Linda."

Carmen happily replies "ok, it will be my pleasure!"

Just then Brian and Bradley come walking up.

Katy says "hey! I heard you guys tried to help Linda's husband. That was very brave of you! Can I ask you guys to do me a favor?"

"Sure! What is it?" Bradley responds.

"Escort me to the Arena! I will fill you in along the way!"

As they ride in the cab Brian asks "ok, why are we going to the Arena?!"

Katy replies, "I'm doing a favor for Carmen. She is a part time lady wrestler."

Bradley says "ok! How can you help?"

Katy sighs, "go to YouTube and search Gorgeous Katy wrestling!"

Brian and Bradley both scroll through YouTube then Brian says "holy crap! You're a wrestler? That's freaking awesome! I had you pegged as an HR supervisor who constantly tells people to use proper pronouns and stuff!"

Katy laughs, "OMG! No way!"

They arrive at the Arena.

Bradley tells Katy, "This is so exciting! I hope you're pretty good!"

"We shall see! Now let's find Matilda!", she responds.

Brian uses his junior high school Spanish, and they are directed into an office. As soon as they walk in a lady walks up and shakes Katy's hand. She says "hello Katy! I'm Matilda, Carmen has told me all about you. You must be a special kind of person to be willing to fill in for someone that you barely know. Now I will give your friends some ringside seats while we go into the dressing room and talk."

Brian and Bradley take the tickets and leave.

Matilda takes Katy to the dressing room and informs her that she is taking on Lucia Loca. Matilda says "in English that means Crazy Lucy! She is tough but beatable. Your problem isn't her but the crew she is with. They are called Las Brujas Malvadas! The Evil Witches! Their leader is Pazia Ponderosa. Powerful Pazia. She has been pounding on all the good girls for years now. So, if you beat Lucia, you will have a target on your back."

Katy laughs, "hmm I came here to get a break from a feud. But ok! Carmen needs this win and I've never backed down from a challenge!"

Matilda says "wow! You're a tiger! I will be ringside cheering you on!"

Katy puts on her Pink Princess outfit and struggles to adjust the mask. She waits in the back until she hears the announcement "ahora caminando hacia el ring… Princesa Rosada!"

Katy strolls to the ring shocked by how much the people love her character! She gets in the ring and sees Lucia Loca run right at her! Katy darts out of the way and Lucia crashes into the corner. The bell rings and the two ladies go right at it! Katy takes Lucia to the mat with an arm drag. Katy really applies the pressure as Lucia stomps the mat in pain! The crowd chants "Princesa! Princesa!" Lucia reaches up and twists Katy's mask making it hard for Katy to see. Katy releases the arm hold and tries to fix her mask when Lucia pops up and kicks Katy in the midsection! Brian and Bradley both yell "oh man! That hurt!" Katy doubles over and Lucia hits her with a knee lift! Ouch! Katy crashes to the mat! The crowd boos as Lucia runs and springs off the ropes! Lucia leaps in the air to crash down on Katy! But whoa! Katy rolls away and Lucia slams to the mat knocking the wind out of her! Katy leans on the ropes catching her breath as Lucia staggers to her feet. The two ladies meet in the center of the ring and lock up. The match turns into a crash course in the Lucha Libre Mexican style wrestling for Katy. The crowd is on the edge of their seats as Katy adapts and withstands the challenge. Finally, Katy is able to catch Lucia with a flying head scissor! She takes Lucia to the mat with a victory roll. She has Lucia's legs hooked as she sits on her chest. Katy holds tight while the ref counts Uno! Dos! Y...... Tres!! Katy gets the 1,2,3!! The crowd lets out a collective cheer!!

"La granadora es Princesa Rosada!!"

But Katy's joy is short lived when she gets back to the dressing room and is met by the Las Brujas Malvadas!

Pazia grabs Katy and says "I know you're not Carmen. You're an American, I can tell by the way you wrestle. You don't come here and embarrass us. I've already spoken with the promoter, and we are having a match next time. Myself and two of my crew against you and two other masked ladies. I got to determine the stakes. If your team loses you all get unmasked and get your heads shaved. That means the Pink Princess will be no more! If we lose, which we won't, your team gets our pay for the night and new wrestling outfits."

Katy declares "I don't have anyone I will need time to talk with some of the ladies here."

Pazia roars "too bad it's on! You can always forfeit then take your punishment in the ring." Katy sternly replies "I'd never do that! You're on Pazia! I will find people!"

The witches storm off and Brian and Bradley rush in.

Bradley says "wow! That was incredible. We thought you were a goner like 5 times!"

Katy laughs, "I know! This Mexican style of wrestling is very different."

Then Matilda walks in, "Katy! You did great! I really thought you would lose but didn't want to say anything! Great job! But I just heard about your upcoming match! I will try to get you some help. It will be hard because everyone is afraid of the Brujas!"

Katy sighs, "Thank you Matilda but we need to get back to the resort and help Linda! This fight with Pazia will have to wait."

They arrive at the resort and Katy is so happy to be done listening to Brian and Bradley go on and on about the match during the car ride back. Linda comes running up to Katy "The police got a note from the kidnappers!"

Katy asks, "ok, when do we leave?!"

Linda answers, "first thing in the morning."

Then Linda looks Katy up and down, "wow! You should get some sleep Katy you look like you were hit by a bus!"

Katy smiles, "a nice hot bath to soothe my muscles then yes lots of sleep! A great night's sleep!" Bright and early the next morning Katy is at the front desk talking with Carmen who can't thank Katy enough for what she did.

"Katy, I will call every lady I know to team up with you. I'm so sorry that you have to deal with Pazia she is terrible."

"Not the first time a crazy competitor has been out to get me! But I would really like to keep my hair!"

Just then Linda walks up all nervous. Carmen greets her with "Hello Miss Linda, your cab is here. I will pray that everything works out."

Katy holds Linda's hand all the way to the Police Headquarters. When they arrive Captain Lopez promptly welcomes them and escorts them into his office.

"We received this letter, and they say your husband has been treated very well and they even had him write you a quick note." Captain Lopez shows the note to Linda.

It simply states, "I love you Linda and I always will."

Linda starts to sob, "this is definitely Anthony's handwriting."

The Captain says "oh, very good. Now this is what the kidnappers want. They are demanding you contact Anthony's father and obtain all the information that he has on the Kinger mine in Idaho."

Linda is confused, "what? Why? Anthony has nothing to do with it. But I will call Anthony's dad right away."

Captain Lopez suggests, "ok, please get on that right away. But I promise you that we are putting pressure on every informant that we have. I really want to make an example of these guys. This crap has to stop once and for all."

Katy thanks the Captain and they leave to go back to the resort. On the way back Linda is an emotional wreck.

Katy hugs her, "hey! Anthony is still alive. They just want info on some mine. It's just about money! We will get him back I promise. Now when we get back you call Anthony's dad, and I will do a deep dive into what the heck that mine is all about."

Katy goes online and learns that the Kinger mine has a deposit of rare earth metals that would be able to compete with China.

"Whoa, that could be huge. It must be all about money. I wonder what Anthony's dad found out and why it's worth kidnapping someone over?" She thinks out loud.

There is a knock on the door. Katy opens it and Linda is there with a stack of papers that Anthony's dad faxed to her. Katy reads all about how there are rare earth metals, but Anthony's dad had an environmental impact report that states if they attempt to mine the metals the entire water supply to the Pacific Northwest could be affected.

"Damn! I knew it was all about money." Katy exclaims, "I guarantee someone, or some group wants to bury that report in order to make insane profits. They definitely want Anthony's dad to keep quiet or else."

"Mike, Anthony's dad will do whatever they say." Linda tells Katy.

"Good. But who is behind this? I'm going to have to ask Mike about who all knows about this environmental report?"

"Ok but he is all upset. Let's get this information to Captain Lopez and see how that goes." Katy agrees. They fax everything to Captain Lopez and he replies back saying "great job! We were told where to leave the information and then we have to wait for their next move."

He tells Katy to take care of Linda and try to keep her occupied. So, Katy takes Linda to the front desk and they talk with Carmen. She reserved them a sailboat loaded with drinks.

Carmen tells Katy, "Please go have fun. I'm still trying to get you some tag team partners" Katy laughs in reply, "oh! That's right! Those evil witches! I will worry about that later. Now it's time for the sun and the sea."

Just as she finishes Brian and Bradley walk up.

"You ladies are speaking our language! Let's go!" Brian says, hinting for an invite.

Katy rolls her eyes and says "ok, ok!"

They sail along the shore staying close to the resort while Brian and Bradley bicker about who the Captain is.

Katy hands Linda a drink, "I know this is awful, but everyone is doing their best. You shouldn't feel guilty at all for trying to get a few minutes of peace to clear your mind. I don't know Anthony but I'm pretty sure he knows you are doing everything you can and would want you to take a break and collect your thoughts."

Linda, in turn, gives Katy a hug and sips her drink. Katy lays on the deck trying to catch a tan when Bradley walks over and stands above her.

"Excuse me you're blocking my sun." Katy tells him.

"Oh sorry! I just wanted to show you there are two dolphins off the port bow. Just a cool scene I thought." Bradley explains.

Katy peeks up and Brian squirts her with a super soaker! Katy jumps up and pushes both Brian and Bradley overboard. Katy laughs as they both shout "hey! We are from Iowa! We aren't the best swimmers."

Katy laughs and throws them a life ring. Linda jumps up and says "that's the best thing I've seen in a while. Thank you, all, ha, ha!"

The guys clumsily climb back in the boat.

"I'm glad to be of service! Hee, hee!" Katy manages to say in between laughs.

They spend the next hour just talking and laughing about all the misadventures they all have had in their lives. Katy looks at her watch and tells the guys to head back in.

"This was so great," she says, "but we need to get back to business."

Katy and Linda go and use the computer in the business media room by the front desk when they get a call from Captain Lopez. He informs them that the kidnappers reviewed all the information, and they demand that Mr. Wagner destroy every copy of the report in his possession. Then they will send him a new report that they want submitted to the EPA. Once he does that, they will inform the Captain when they will release Anthony.

Katy gasps, "I freaking knew it. It's all about greed! To hell with the environment. All hail, the all-mighty dollar!"

Linda immediately runs off to tell Anthony's dad. Katy gets on the computer and does a full work up on Mike Wagner.

Katy says to herself "why would Mr. Wagner be so involved in an environmental impact study? He must do more than Linda thinks and I'm going to find out what."

After a bit of searching, it seems that the Enormous Fund placed Micheal Wagner in charge of overseeing the process of making the Kinger mine operational.

Linda returns, "Mike will do whatever it takes."

Katy responds, "I hate this but that's great. Anthony is way more important than the mine. But once he is safely in your arms then I will see to it that the mine never pollutes a drop of water."

The next morning Katy is up early and goes for a run. Afterwards she is at the bar enjoying a mimosa when Carmen slowly walks over still favoring that ankle.

"Good morning, Miss Katy. I have some bad news. Your match against the Brujas is tonight. Pazia got it switched to really put you at a disadvantage. Also, I couldn't find any ladies here in Mexico to be your partners."

"What? Tonight? Well, that's terrible but I'm not backing down. I guess I will take them on alone."

Carmen puts her hand on Katy's shoulder, "you're so brave! So fearless! I'm so sorry I couldn't find any Mexican ladies, but I did find these two!"

Katy looks over to where Carmen gestures and in walks Izzy and Jenny! Katy is in complete disbelief! She immediately jumps to her feet and gives them both a huge hug!

"OMG! I can't believe it! What are you guys doing here?!" Katy yells with joy.

"Carmen got Ray's number from her boss." Izzy tells her, "He isn't happy about you being involved in a mess but that's a story for another time. He immediately called us and we knew we had to come help our girl!"

Jenny chimes in, "yeah, Ray even paid for our plane tickets. So, what's this all about?!"

Katy asks them to sit down, "I'm sure you're hungry."

They order food and Katy tells them what's going on, "How does this happen? You all know I came down for a little vacation when this lady Linda's husband got kidnapped! Then on top of that, Carmen, who you met, is also a wrestler and was injured so I filled in for her and now I'm in a serious bind!"

Jenny urges her to continue "tell us what this match is."

Katy says, "there is this lady Pazia, the head of a group of girls called Las Brujas Malvadas!" Izzy chimes in, "oh! The evil witches!"

"Yes!" Katy replies, "I beat their friend so now I have to face them in a 6-lady tag team match! We are the masked good girls. I'm the Pink Princess and you two can pick your names."

Jenny is enthusiastic but wants to know more. "Ok cool but Carmen mentioned something about a special stipulation?"

"Oh… that." Now, Katy says sheepishly, "Yes. If we lose, we get our heads shaved and we get unmasked. Apparently in Mexico that's a huge disgrace." And then she continues, with more confidence in her voice, "But if we win, we get their pay and new outfits."

Jenny's face sinks, "oh", she says, "whoa! I'm ok with being unmasked but I don't want to go back to work bald. Oh man! I gotta think about this."

Izzy perks right up, "don't worry Katy! I'm with you win or lose!"

Now Jenny is feeling a bit guilty and says "I'm sorry Katy you've done so much for me. I'm in too."

Katy, with tears in her eyes, tells the both of them, "I love you girls! You have no idea how much this means to me!"

They laugh and Katy tells them how the match will go, and they all come up with some great strategies.

Izzy and Jenny go take a nap to recover from the flight while Katy meets up with Linda. She tells Katy that Mike received the fake report and will submit it to the EPA.

Linda tells Katy, "Mining will begin in two days."

Katy nods, "Ok, now let's get Anthony back and then we'll try to stop that mine from opening. We can do it!"

Katy calls Captain Lopez and tells him that Mike received the report and will submit it to the EPA right away. She asks him to immediately let them know when they hear anything from the kidnappers.

Captain Lopez says "absolutely!"

Katy tells Linda that things are looking good. Linda takes a seat and starts to cry.

Katy soothes, "hey no crying. This nightmare will soon be over. Have you eaten anything? I'm sure you haven't. Let's get you some food."

"Did you drop from heaven?" Linda asks Katy with sincerity, "Who are you? You're incredible. I was talking with Carmen about your match, and I told her that if you couldn't find anyone that the least I could do was get in the ring and stand by your side."

Katy looks at Linda and says "really? You were willing to get in there untrained and take on those ladies with me?!"

Linda replies "yes! I have no idea what I was going to do but I was going to be there for you!" Katy simply says, "Thank you!"

Izzy and Jenny wake from their nap and hit the gym. They take it easy just doing light cardio and muscle stretches. Katy joins them and does the same.

"So? Any ideas on what your wrestler names will be?", Katy asks.

Izzy says "I will be La Escorpion Roja! The Red Scorpion!"

Jenny says "I asked Izzy, and we came up with La Bomba Azul! The Blue Bombshell."

"Those are perfect. Again, I can't thank you guys enough."

The ladies finish working out and Katy gets a text from Carmen: "Hello, Miss Katy, all the ladies who I wrestle with are so sorry that they are too afraid to take on the Brujas. But they sent over quite the collection of masks and outfits that will be perfect for your friends."

Katy tells the girls, "Hey! After we are done here, you guys get showered up. Carmen has a bunch of outfits and masks to try on. This should be cool."

An excited Izzy comments, "yes! I can't wait.".

A more conservative Jenny says, "I just hope I look good and that the mask fits. I've never wrestled in one."

Katy tells her, "Yeah, the mask is important. Loca Lucia twisted mine and got me pretty good as I tried to fix it."

At that moment, Linda walks in, "I'd love to see you ladies perform but I will be staying here just in case I get a call. But I will be thinking of you and praying hard!"

Katy turns to Linda "we really appreciate your support. We know you have to stay here. I'm still so touched that you offered to help. Please just relax and I know things will be ok. I have a good feeling."

Katy tries to leave when Brian and Bradley come running up!

"Umm, aren't you gonna introduce us to your friends?! Tell them that our dad is rich!", Brain eagerly asks.

Katy laughs, "hey Izzy grab Jenny, I want you to meet my new friends who despite their goofball antics have been a big help."

Jenny and Izzy look them up and down and Izzy says, "you guys remind me a lot of my good friend Tommy."

Bradley grins, "well I would love to be your very, very close and intimate friend."

Izzy raps him in the gut and feigns a look of disgust, "men! You guys are all crazy."

Brian yells as the ladies walk away, "don't forget to tell us when you're heading to the Arena. We wouldn't miss the match for anything in the world."

Katy shouts back "ok! I will let you guys know."

They all arrive at the Arena. Even Brian and Bradley made it against Izzy's better judgement. The guys get their tickets and head to the seats. Matilda greets them and escorts them to the dressing room. She tells them the goal of the match.

She says "this is probably a match that none of you have had. The goal is the first team to score three pins on the other team and then score a submission on the other team will be the winner. It's a long and tough match."

Jenny's face turns to a look of worry, "that's seems so difficult. That's a long and tough match!"

Matilda agrees, "yes, it's difficult but you will see things break down and it's a free-for-all and the pins come quickly. The referee kinda lets things go."

Just then Pazia storms in and looks them over. She points at Katy and snorts, "oh! You're the lady from the resort that had the kidnapping. Now that I see your face, you look familiar. I hope you like a bald head and being unmasked as a bunch of American losers. Say your prayers ladies. See you in the ring!"

Izzy yells as Pazia walks away, "thanks for the pep talk we appreciate it ha ha!"

Katy and the ladies get into their outfits. They look into the mirror and laugh.

Izzy critiques, "look at us! We are red, pink and blue superheroes!"

Jenny announces, "I love this outfit, but this mask will take some getting used to."

Katy puts each arm around their waists and declares "this will be a war! But I have my two best friends at my side. If things go wrong, I will beg Pazia to just shave my head. She might go for that."

Izzy has the final say, "No! We win as a team, or we lose as a team. But we won't lose!"

The ladies peek at the ring from the back as the ring announcer booms over the mic, "Las Brujas Malvadas! Irma Implacable! Ruthless Irma! Inez Impresionate! Amazing Inez! Y La Liber de Las Brujas!! Pazia Ponderosa!"

"The leader of the witches Powerful Pazia!", Izzy translates, "ok let's go!"

They walk towards the ring as the announcer continues to shout, "caminando hacia el ring Las Damas Valientes! Princesa Rosada! La Escorpion Roja! Y La Bomba Azul!"

The crowd goes absolutely nuts as they wave to the crowd! Katy brings Izzy and Jenny in close and says "I love you two no matter what! But let's spank these witches!"

Katy and Pazia start things off. Pazia charges at Katy and Katy slides to the right as Pazia flies past her and collides with the ropes. Katy follows right behind her kneeing Pazia in the back as she bounces off. Pazia falls to the mat and the crowd cheers! Pazia gets up in a rage but is immediately leveled by a clothesline! Irma runs in and hits Katy from behind. Izzy leaps over the ropes and nails Irma with a dropkick! Inez comes in screaming and attacks Izzy! Jenny enters the fray and yanks Inez off Izzy. It's a full-on melee until the referee finally gets control. The match turns into a tag team battle like no other. Quick tags, lots of saves, and plenty of cheating by the Brujas. Finally, Izzy catches Irma with a spinning neck breaker. Pazia dives in to stop the pin but Katy drop kicks her into the corner! The ref counts 1,2,3!! The crowd goes crazy as The Courageous Ladies win the first fall! But their joy is short lived as all three Brujas trap Izzy and pummel her in the corner. Jenny runs in but gets spears by Inez! They body slam Izzy to the mat and both Pazia and Irma prepare to leap off the top rope and demolish Izzy. Katy flies in and stands over Izzy protecting her from a double set of flying missile dropkicks! Katy takes the double kicks full force and is practically driven through the mat! Irma stomps on Izzy as Inez holds Jenny back. Pazia covers Katy as the ref counts 1,2,3!!!

The crowd boos as the Brujas have tied the score!

Again, the match resumes to a heated tag team encounter until Jenny and Inez tie each other up in double small package. The ref counts 1,2,3!!! Both ladies pop up and there is total confusion. Finally, the ref indicates that both ladies pinned the other, so each team gets a loss and a win! The crowd is on their feet. What a match! So once again it's all tied up! Since Jenny and Inez must start things back up Inez quickly whips Jenny into the corner where Pazia and Irma are waiting. They choke and kick her mercilessly until Katy and Izzy fly in and save Jenny. The ref argues with Katy as Izzy drags Jenny to safety. But from behind Pazia and Inez annihilate Katy with a simultaneous knee strike and clothesline! Wow! Izzy turns to help Katy but gets hit with a high cross body block from Irma. Pazia leaps up and hits Katy with a giant splash! Pazia again covers Katy as the ref counts 1,2,3!!! Oh no!! The Brujas now lead 3 -2! All they need is a submission to win! Izzy takes Katy to their corner and tells her "That's it! You can't take anymore! They are targeting you!" Katy struggles but says "no! I got this!" Katy and Pazia meet to continue the match. Katy lets out a scream and unloads on Pazia! She is stunned as Katy whips her into the ropes! Pazia bounces off and is flattened by Katy's flying double knee strike to her chest! Pazia slams to the mat with the wind completely knocked out of her! Katy wraps her up in tight cradle as the ref counts 1,2,3!!!! Katy did it! The match is all tied up! It happened so fast that Irma and Inez didn't have time to make the save! Pazia is pounding the mat and throwing a fit! The crowd is delirious!

This is it. Whichever team gets a submission now will be the winner. Katy and Pazia lock up but Irma and Inez jump in and start to pound on Katy! Izzy and Jenny enter and it's an all-out brawl. All six ladies are flying around the ring trying to finish each other off. The crowd can't keep up with all the action! Eventually the Brujas evil tactics take control. They have the Courageous Ladies down on the mat. Irma and Inez put Jenny and Izzy into Boston Crab submission holds! They are face to face in agony as Irma and Inez try to fold them in half. Meanwhile Pazia has Katy trapped in a figure four leg lock! Jenny looks at Izzy and goes to slap the mat in submission. Izzy grabs her hand before it hits the mat and says "hang on! Hang on!" Just then the bell rings and Irma and Inez release their holds and dance around the ring claiming victory! Jenny says to Izzy "oh no! Pazia must have beaten poor Katy!" Then they see Irma and Inez fall to the knees pounding the mat! Izzy and Jenny struggle to their feet and see the referee raise Katy's hand! They run over and the ref says "Princesa Rosada reversed the figure four and Pazia was trapped and gave up!"

They pick Katy off the mat and they all hug and cry!

Katy cries, "I love you guys! We did it"

The crowd goes insane as the ring announcer proclaims, "Las Ganadoras del Partido... Las Damas Valientes! The winners of the match. The Courageous Ladies!!"

Back in the dressing room they just sit back and groan in pain. Jenny says "this is unbelievable. I can't describe what I'm feeling!".

"I know!", Izzy agrees, "I've had a lot of matches but none like this."

Matilda walks in saying, "ladies that was the best match we've had here in 20 years! I'm still shaking!"

Matilda then announces, "you guys have a visitor.", when in walks Pazia!

"Here is the money you ladies won, plus I'm leaving a card for our costume maker to make you guys whatever outfits you want. I just want to say you are some of the best wrestlers I've ever seen. We cheated and abused you. But you ladies earned that victory!"

Pazia then points at Katy and says "I thought I knew you! You're Gorgeous Katy! I've seen a few of your matches! You're incredible. So, you've earned my respect and I'm here to help you. My cousin knows the guys who kidnapped that man. I will call him, and they will release him and provide you with everything you need to nail the real person responsible. All they want is to disappear untouched. Do we have a deal?"

Katy is in shock. She goes up to Pazia and says "wow! Really? You're amazing. I will inform Captain Lopez. I'm sure your plan will be acceptable. Thank you so much. I can't believe it Pazia you're actually a good guy!"

Pazia gives a hearty laugh, "if you ever tell anyone that I will find you in a dark alley and beat you down! Ha ha!".

They share a brief hug and Pazia walks away.

Katy gets all cleaned up and calls Captain Lopez. She tells him all that happened.

Captain Lopez asks Katy "how in the world did you get to speak with Pazia?! She is a crazy wrestler who is also a big shot in Mexican organized crime!"

"We had a wrestling match."

Lopez in total shock, "you did what? With her? And you're alive to talk about it? I don't want to know anymore. I can't believe it. But yes, we won't go after the kidnappers now but I will find them after all this is finished. Tell Pazia it's a deal."

Katy texts the number that Pazia gave her with Captain Lopez's permission for this exchange to move forward. Katy immediately gets a response.

"Ok", Pazia tells Katy, "Anthony is in a trunk of a car at the corner of Verde Street and La Flora Blvd. He is ok and has everything you need to arrest the person behind all of this." Captain Lopez picks up Katy and they go to the intersection. They see the car and a note on the trunk with the keys. Lopez opens the trunk and there, all tied up, is Anthony. They pull him out and untie him.

"I'm so happy to see you.' Katy tells him. "Linda has been a rock through all this. She loves you!"

Anthony squints. His eyes have to adjust to the sunlight, "thank you! Do I know you?!"

Katy says "yes, we briefly met at the resort."

Now that he can see a bit better, Anthony answers, "that's right! But oh yeah. There is a folder in the trunk for the police with all the information they need. These guys hated the guy who hired them so they took his money and now hope he goes to jail".

Captain Lopez takes the folder and tells Katy to take Anthony back to the resort, "Get him to his wife. I will talk to him tomorrow."

Katy and Anthony arrive back at the resort. They see Bradley and Brian at the lobby bar talking Izzy and Jenny's head off about how that was the greatest thing they have ever seen. Izzy sees Katy and she and Jenny run right up to her.

Jenny says "these guys never shut up! They are crazy!"

Katy laughs, "yes! Yes, they are!"

Katy uses the lobby phone and calls Linda, "Linda we are back from our match. Can you come to the lobby I need your help."

"Absolutely, I'm on my way!"

A minute later Linda comes walking up and sees Anthony. She runs full speed into his arms. She kisses and hugs him and starts to cry! She squeezes him tight and won't let go!

"I can't believe it! You're here! You're alive!"

"I'm ok my love." Anthony tells her, "Apparently, your friend Katy here got someone to convince those guys to let me go."

Linda hugs Katy, "OMG! Katy, You're incredible. We owe you everything. You have a friend for life now! Anything you ever need please don't hesitate to call me."

Katy replies, "I'm so happy to have been able to help. Now I'm going to get drunk with my friends then take a long hot shower and go to bed!"

Izzy yells "hey Bradley! Get us a round of shots! Let's party!"

The next morning Captain Lopez is at the resort restaurant when Katy walks up.

He informs Katy, "The person responsible is a Mr. Wellington Schmidt, he is the silent owner of the Enormous Group. He found out about the environmental impact report and knew he would lose billions. He planned everything, the kidnapping, the false report, and his secret deal with China to sell everything to them. I contacted the FBI and the EPA. They are arresting Mr. Schmidt as we speak, and the EPA is going to make sure that mine never opens. You're a hero Miss Katy."

Katy smiles, "I'm so happy everything worked out. But this was supposed to be my vacation to get away from all this crime and intrigue. Oh well!"

Then she feels a hug from behind. It's Carmen,

"Miss Katy, you saved my wrestling career. Princesa Rosada is all over the Mexican wrestling social media sites. I can't thank you enough. But I have a message for you. Mr. Enzo says since you didn't want to relax, he wants you back in the office. Apparently, the Ukrainian government is sending its valuable artwork to the art museum in your town for safekeeping. He was hired by the museum to come up with a security plan to make sure that the Russian government or anyone else can't steal it. He says there is probably nothing to worry about, but he needs you back home."

Katy does her famous fourth wall break as she smiles and says "ha! Nothing to worry about huh? Nobody will ever steal the artwork huh?"

"Back in the USSR" by the Beatles begins to play!

KATY'S MASTERPIECE

It's been a month since Cozumel and so much has changed.

Izzy is back from her Canadian wrestling tour and has moved back in with Katy.

Jenny is now living with Rob Hamilton. Her friendship with Katy has become a bit strained.

Katy is sitting at her desk when Ray Enzo walks in, "Katy, you're never gonna believe it. Remember when the Art Museum hired us to come up with a security plan to safeguard the Ukrainian art collection?"

"Yes! But they didn't listen and didn't want to spend the money. Why? What happened?!"

"Remember that painting of Marshal Ivan Konev?!"

"Yeah?! The one that is allegedly covering up the famous missing Raphael painting of 'Portrait of a Young Man'. What about it?"

"It was freaking stolen! Now the Feds are involved and so is that idiot, Franklin. So, the museum really wants us to help with this. They are now willing to pay us the big bucks! It hasn't been released to the press and they really want this solved fast to avoid an international incident!"

Katy nods her head in excitement as she says to Ray, "I knew this would happen! Ok let's get right on this."

"Great! I will find out what I can from the Feds and see what Franklin and Sanders are up to regarding this. You go to the museum and speak to the director." Ray tells her.

Katy says, "sounds good. I will keep you posted."

Katy arrives at the Museum and meets the director, Lawrence Lockwood. He greets her and takes her into his office.

"I don't understand it. Everything seemed fine." Mr. Lockwood asserts." I didn't go with all your recommendations because the artwork was kept out of the news. We just blended all the pieces with our portraits. No one was the wiser."

Katy cynically responds, "someone apparently knew. You have heard the rumors that the Portrait of Ivan Konev was just to cover up the missing Raphael piece, right?"

"There have been hundreds of stories about that Raphael painting. I don't believe it's behind Konev's painting at all."

"Ok, but I think someone did. Can I get a list of everyone on your staff so I can do follow up after the police and FBI are finished?"

"Absolutely."

Katy takes the list and starts to review it. She tells Mr. Lockwood that she will be contacting him and will set up dates and times for interviews. He thanks her for coming and says, "please, I beg you and everyone involved in this case to get that painting back. The reputation of this Museum hangs in the balance."

Katy reassures him with a, "don't worry Sir, I'm on the case. Justice will prevail."

Katy is back at her apartment when Izzy walks in.

"Welp, I got another caper!" Katy exclaims.

"Really? What's going on now?" Izzy asks.

"Someone stole a Ukrainian painting from the Art Museum. It's a painting that is rumored to be hiding the famous missing Raphael piece."

Izzy thinks and asks, "what do you think? Did someone know that and that's why it's gone?" Katy replies, "I'm not sure yet if it's that or it could just be the Russians causing trouble."

A laughing Izzy says "I know you will get to the bottom of it. Whoever took it is in real trouble. The FBI and LT Franklin will be running around in circles while you will already have the person caught."

Katy smiles, "I hope so! I would love to solve this one! It would really be a huge deal for Ray's investigative agency."

"I have total faith in you. But now let's talk about Jenny. I text her and she barely responds back. What's really going with her?" a concerned Izzy asks Katy.

Katy sighs, "I'm really bummed about this. She is so upset that her ex-husband is now super successful. She was the one who supported him while he was in school. Then as soon as he graduated, he left her. Now he is making a great amount of money while she is working for the power company!

It must be tough on her. To top things off last week, as you know, Jenny and I lost that tag team match to the Wholesome Twins. They have been on a mission ever since you and I beat them when we wore those masked costumes."

"Yeah, what happened with that match?" Izzy asks.

Katy's face sinks. "They were on fire. It was a pitched battle. We were totally on the defensive. Then Jenny got caught by Patience in a Fujiwara arm bar! You know that move. Your arm can easily be popped right out of the socket. I tried to reach her for a tag but she was too far away. I tried to scream encouragement to her but she had no choice but to submit! Prudence posted a picture of me consoling Jenny in the center of the ring while the Wholesome Twins were standing over us with their arms raised in victory! Jenny was so upset. She said I should have dove in and saved her. The Twins didn't cheat. We would have lost all credibility as a good girl team if I ran in and broke that up. I'd rather lose fair and square than cheat. Jenny didn't see it that way. So those two things put together, the match and the ex-husband have her all torn up."

Izzy sighs and gives Katy a hug, "losing a big match is hard and what Prudence did with that picture is insulting. But I know all that too well from my Canadian tour. But she needs to get over it. Plus, she is with Rob now. He is a great guy. He is totally in love with her. She has it pretty good now."

Katy agrees "I'm still kinda upset about all this too. We were like sisters in the Air Force, I really want to help her get past this."

"I know you will help her Katy, you're the most kind and caring person I know."

Katy is in the office bright and early and starts to research some of the names on the list that Mr. Lockwood gave her. The security guard, Clay Jamison, has really bad credit and was fired from his last two jobs.

Katy murmurs to herself "hmm, I wonder if Mr. Lockwood knows about that?"

Next, she is examining Wallace Vanderman. His position says he is an Aesthetician.

Katy thinks, "Aesthetician? What's that?"

She googles it and discovers it's a person who is an expert in the appreciation of beauty, especially in art.

"Oh, that's interesting," She thinks out loud, as Ray walks in.

"Lay off researching those people for now. The FBI and the Police will beat that horse to death. We need to think outside of the box and look in places where they won't. My plan is to snoop around just enough so they keep their eyes on me which leaves you able to find that missing link."

"Ok! I like that idea." Katy tells Ray, "They will be too busy worrying about what you're doing to pay me any mind. That leaves me free range to do what I do."

Ray shakes his head, "oh boy! That kinda scares me! Just be careful please!"

"Don't you worry about a thing."

Ray just laughs and walks away.

The wheels in Katy's head begin to spin. She finally comes up with Dimitri Metroff.

"Well, I can't go by Kirov Koffee but I bet I can find out where he eats." Katy thinks.

She again taps the keys on her computer and finds the only Russian restaurant in town. "Tatiana's!!" Katy says as she runs out the door.

She arrives at the restaurant and sees Dimitri sitting in the back corner. As she makes her way over to the table she is immediately stopped by a massive brute. Viktor. When Dimitri looks up and sees what's going on he quickly waves Viktor off and lets Katy sit down. In his heavy Russian accent, he says "ahh! Miss America! This is going to be interesting. Why are you here?"

"A painting of Marshal Konev has been stolen from the art museum. What do you know about it?", Katy asks.

Dimitri pretends to give her a hurt look, "Always right to the point. Never any idle chit chat with you. No hello Dimitri, how's the food here?"

"I want answers! This is a really big deal that could have international repercussions. If you don't tell me what I want to know, then I will be forced to act." Katy shouts in the toughest voice she can muster.

This set Dimitri into a fit of laughter.

"Are you really trying to threaten me again?!", he howls.

With that, Viktor takes his one meat hook of a hand and squeezes the back of Katy's neck. Dimitri stops him with a casual wave, still chuckling, he tells Viktor, "No Viktor it's ok. This is entertainment. Alright Miss. America, threaten away!"

Katy rubs her neck and says to the grinning Dimitri, "I don't know how much you know about art but there has always been a rumor that the painting is actually covering something much more valuable."

"Ah, the 'Portrait of a Young Man'." Dimitri answers with humor in his eyes.

Katy's gives him a look of astonishment.

"Yes! How did you know that? Did you steal it ?!"

Dimitri lets out an exasperated sigh. "Miss America, I know all about the Great Patriotic War that you Americans call World War Two. I also know all the stories about the painting. I've had the KGB and my friend Sergei and now you ask me the same question. I will tell you what I told them. No, I didn't take it but now that I know it's out there, I'm going to recover it for the good of the people. Why? Because I'm a noble businessman."

Puzzled, Katy asks, "ok but what if the 'Portrait of a Young Man' is underneath?"

Dimitri once again laughs and says "Vladimir Putin would love to have it in his private collection. But I'm sure the stories about the painting are completely false. Now I'm busy.

Viktor escort her out please."

Viktor and his meat hook, pick up Katy and not too gently shows her the door.

Katy adjusts herself.

"I'm pretty sure he didn't steal it." She thinks. "But now he wants to get his hands on it, so that could be trouble."

Just then Katy gets a text from Izzy: "hey, stop by the bar. I've got some news for you."

Katy enters the bar and sees Izzy back at her old job serving drinks and making people laugh.

"It just feels right with you at the helm of this place." She tells Izzy. "So what's the news?"

Izzy informs Katy of the news, "I spoke with Jenny, and she will be here soon. She has something for us to consider."

"Oh good. I really want to see her." Katy says.

The door opens and LT Franklin and Detective Sanders walk in and approach Katy.

"I know the museum has you and Enzo looking into this art caper, but stay out of our way. Make sure you tell Ray that we are keeping an eye on him. Nothing gets past me. I'm going to show you and the FBI that I'm the best investigator around here." Franklin scolds.

Detective Sanders taps Katy on the shoulder as they walk away, "ha! Don't worry about him. He fears you! You got him rattled."

Izzy agrees, "see Katy, you're the best. Oh wow! Here comes Jenny."

Katy immediately gives Jenny a huge hug.

"Geez, Jenny, I missed you. How are you?"

"I'm fine. I have a proposition for you guys," Jenny says, getting right to the point.

Katy says, "we're all ears! Shoot!"

"Tomorrow night there is this all-ladies Battle Royal that I took the liberty to sign us up for. The winner or winners get 5 thousand dollars. I know if we work together, we can totally win this thing. We can wear the new outfits that those Mexican ladies made for us. What do you guys think?"

Izzy is the first to comment, "Battle Royals are crazy and anything can happen."

Katy is surprised by Jenny's invitation. "Really? I thought you were mad at me and wanted to take a break from us working together?"

"No way Katy!" Jenny reassures her. "We are friends. You have nothing to worry about. I just think this will be so good for us."

"Ok, we're in." Katy beams.

Then, suddenly, Rob Hamilton walks up and says "I'm so glad that you ladies are talking. It makes me feel good. Now let me take my champion out to dinner. You ladies have fun but don't stay out too late."

As Rob and Jenny take their leave, Izzy grabs Katy and whispers in her ear, "something seems off. You've known her a lot longer than I have but I think she is up to something."

Katy tells Izzy "I felt that too but no way. We've been friends for way too long. We've been through way too much. She is still just a little off kilter over her ex-husband."

Ray texts Katy: "wake up sleepy head meet me at the diner."

Katy gets dressed and meets up with Ray.

"What's up? Why aren't we meeting at the office?" Kay asks.

Ray explains, "I'm being followed so I want to make it look like we're up to something clandestine. I need you after breakfast to head to the abandoned shoe factory while I go check out some pawn shops. They will be wondering what the heck we are up to. After that I will go the library and do "research" on art while you go to the University and talk to the art department. That will keep them guessing. Then just hit the gym like you always do."

"That's a great idea. Professor Conway will talk my ear off about art for an hour at least."

They finish breakfast and split up. Ray does his thing while Katy swings by the shoe factory then goes by Gunness University. At the school, Katy reminisces about all the good times that she had there. After a stroll down memory lane, she knocks on the office door of Professor Conway.

The Professor calls out, "is that Katy Rachford? You're like the most famous person to ever come out of this school. Albeit not for your academics which were stellar but for being a fighting superhero. How can I help you?"

"Oh thank you," Katy, replies a bit embarrassed. "But I'm no superhero. I'm just someone who got involved in a crazy, thrilling, and competitive experience. But I could use your help with the history of the lost art from World War Two."

Professor Conway is more than happy to discuss, "what an awful time in world history. So many masterpieces were lost to evil people. But it's funny that you mention that, because about two weeks ago a man who I never met was asking about the 'Portrait of a Young Man' painting and what might have happened to it."

Katy's interest peaks, "did he give his name? Can you describe him?"

"No, he didn't give his name and I wasn't really paying attention to his features. He was an average middle-aged white man."

"That's ok you've been very helpful. Thank you." Katy tells Professor Conway

Professor Conway smiles and says, "You're welcome but I didn't do anything."

Katy picks up Izzy from the bar and asks "where is Jenny?

Izzy replies, "I think Rob is taking her. But I don't feel right about this. I don't know why but I don't."

"It's a bit of a drive to this event so please voice to me all your concerns." Katy tells her.

The ladies talk all the way there and they agree to trust Jenny.

They go to the dressing room and meet Jenny.

"Great! You guys made it!" Jenny seems really pleased to see Katy and Izzy,

"Do you like the outfit those Mexican ladies made me?", she asks her two friends.

Izzy says, "very nice but what's with all the dollar signs all over it?"

Jenny tells her, "I'm Jet-Set Jenny Ryan, I just thought it looked cool."

"I think you look great.", Katy interjects.

Izzy and Katy change into their new outfits and they all look fantastic.

They enter the ring. It's filled with all the local talent. In there is Sally Slick, Marvelous Mindy, Debbie and Donna Doom and Raquel Ruthless. Even Patience and Prudence Wholesome have come to the party. The ringer announcer says, "this is an over-the-top rope Battle Royal! When a lady is thrown over the top rope and hits the floor she is eliminated. The winners or winners get five thousand dollars and…."

As he tries to finish talking all hell breaks loose in the ring. Debbie and Donna Doom toss him out of the ring and it's "go" time. Katy goes right after Prudence and whips her into the corner and nails her with a flying elbow. Izzy body slams Raquel to the mat as Mindy starts to wail on Jenny. Sally and Patience are getting pummeled by the Doom sisters. It's a wild affair with the ladies giving it their all. The crowd is amazed by how fast the action is. Jenny is about to be thrown out of the ring by Mindy when Izzy comes to her rescue and tosses Mindy over to top rope and onto the floor! Wow! Katy takes a groggy Prudence and whips her into the ropes! Katy runs up to Prudence as she bounces off and clotheslines her out of the ring! Prudence has been eliminated! Katy yells "take a picture of that Prudence!" Raquel is choking Patience with the top rope when Izzy and Katy grab their feet and throw them both out of the ring! Izzy and Katy turn around just in time to see Debbie Doom stomping on Sally while Donna has Jenny over her head about to throw her over the rope and onto the floor. Izzy grabs Donna around her waist while Katy grabs Jenny's boot just in time before she sails out of the ring. Jenny recovers in the corner while Katy and Izzy battle it out with Debbie and Patience. It's a good back and forth with Debbie and Patience almost getting the better of Katy and Izzy. Finally, Katy and Izzy rally and catch Debbie and Patience with a double spear to their midsections! Wow! Debbie and Patience had the wind completely knocked out of them. As they are trying to catch their breath Katy and Izzy pick them up and toss them out of the ring!! Debbie and Patience are gone! They pick up Jenny and give her a hug. Katy and Izzy start waving to the crowd when Jenny runs up and mule kicks them square in the back! Katy goes over the top rope and falls to the floor! Izzy is out of the ring but is hanging on to the top rope by her fingernails!! Jenny bites Izzy's fingers and she falls to the floor! OMG! Jenny has betrayed her two best friends! Jet-Set Jenny Ryan wins the Battle Royal! Katy and Izzy pick each other up and look back into the ring in complete shock!

A beaten and battered ring announcer enters the ring, "with a stunning turn of events the winner of the Battle Royal is Jet-Set Jenny Ryan!"

The crowd boos at the top of their lungs!

Jenny snatches the microphone from the ring announcer's hand and yells, "shut up losers! I'm no longer Jet-Set Jenny Ryan. Now, I'm Jenny Moneybags Ryan! I'm all about making cash and kicking ass! Guess what Katy and Isabelle? The ring announcer never got to finish what the winner of the match gets besides the money. I get to schedule a few matches. So, Izzy, you will now have a match with Christine Dream Crusher Caruso! That's right Izzy, the lady who destroyed you and took away your Canadian Ladies Title! As for you Gorgeous Katy you have a match with me. But by the way, I took your first edition autographed copy of Agatha Christie's 'And Then There Were None'. That stupid book that you claim is the greatest mystery novel ever written. If you win you can have it back but if you lose, I will burn it unless you give me twenty-five thousand dollars!"

Katy and Izzy climb back in the ring.

Katy looks at Jenny. There is nothing but utter sadness in her face.

Izzy, however, is fuming. She grabs the microphone and declares in disgust, "I can't believe you Jenny! You're a traitor! Katy has been nothing but good to you. How could you do this? As for Christine? She is a complete monster, but I won't back down!"

Izzy spins around and addresses the on-lookers, "But now I want to talk to the fans. I'm going to start a Go Fund Me page for Katy. God forbid she loses. There is no way I'm going to let her book get burned. I hope you all will try to pitch in and help!"

The crowd yells "we love you, Katy! We love you Izzy!"

Then they start to chant "Katy Go Fund Me! Save that book! Save that book!"

Izzy drives home as Katy slumps in the passenger seat, devastated.

Katy mumbles "I can't believe it. She was like my sister. How did this happen?"

Izzy slaps her knee, "she is blinded by anger and jealousy. She is angry at her ex and jealous of you because you are such a great person and such a great competitor. To her everything comes easy for you. She has no idea how much work you've put in and how you are guided by an amazing moral compass." Then, Izzy's voice rises in anger, "But are you kidding me? Jenny wants to burn your book? Who the hell does she think she is? Some crazy dictator? That's some really nasty stuff right there! Trust me Katy, we will get through this together."

Katy takes Izzy's hand. She cheers up a bit and says, "thank you Izzy! You have been my rock. Please let us make a pact now to never become a Jenny towards each other no matter what!"

Izzy says "Katy my girl! You got it. True blue friends to the end!"

Katy strolls into the building late, for the first time ever. Ray runs up to her. He could see the pain in her expression. He immediately takes her into his office and says "ok, I don't like that look in your face. You're my light and my inspiration. What the heck is going on? Who do I have to hang off the side of a bridge to make this all go away?"

Katy, with tears in her eyes, tells him, "Jenny is so upset with life. She turned on me. We are no longer friends."

Ray is shocked, "what? Why?"

"She is angry about her ex-husband being successful and she is upset that her wrestling career isn't going as well as she thinks it should." Katy tells him in-between sniffles.

"F her! You've done everything for her. Now, I want you to go home and relax. Maybe go do something fun. Catch a movie. Get drunk someplace. Be a rebel and throw a soda can in the regular trash and not in the recycle bin."

This makes Katy laugh. "Thank you. That's pretty funny. You know I'd never put a can in the regular trash! Hee, hee! But no, no. I want to get to work. What are we doing today?"

"Alright, alright, alright! That's my Katy! Always ready, willing, and able! Now I've heard it through the grapevine that the FBI has been putting the screws to that security guard that you were researching. But I don't think he is involved. That's too easy. But the FBI likes it easy. Tell me what happened at the University."

Katy tells Ray what she discovered. "Professor Conway told me a middle-aged white man asked her questions about the 'Portrait of a Young Man'. She had no idea who he was, but she gave him a whole history lesson."

Ray comments, "Conway is extremely book smart but not very street smart. Too bad she didn't pay closer attention to his appearance. But that's ok. I will wander around town to keep Franklin guessing and you go back to the school and talk to Vinny Pira in security. He owes me a few favors. See what you can find on video. Maybe the security cameras got a good view of this guy's face."

"Yes, I hope we beat the FBI and Franklin to the punch."

"I got you, Katy, I know we will."

Katy meets Vinny Pira at the security office, and she starts to review all the video footage from the security camera that covers the main entrance to the Fine Arts building on campus. Katy methodically goes through the footage minute by minute. Vinny hands Katy a pen and paper. He then asks, "hey! Can I get an autograph for my daughter? She is a huge fan."

Katy asks, "you know who I am?"

Vinny answers, "of course! You're Gorgeous Katy! Gunness University's most famous graduate!"

Katy laughs and writes his daughter a nice note.

Katy returns her attention to the videos. She sees several men that could possibly be the subject. She takes a bunch of screenshots and puts them on a thumb drive. She thanks Mr. Pira and proceeds to leave the campus. As she walks to her car, she is stopped by Professor Conway who tells Katy that a Detective Tamara Sanders came by asking about how one painting can be hidden under another and to give her a brief lesson on the stolen art of World War Two.

Professor Conway tells Katy, "I never mentioned you or the middle-aged man. After we talked, Detective Sanders thanked me and left."

Katy says "she is a smart lady. She is definitely on the same track as me. Thank you for the heads up."

Katy swings by the bar and is immediately grabbed by Izzy.

Izzy shows Katy the "Go Fund Me" page that she created on her laptop.

Izzy is ecstatic and tells Katy "It's only been a few hours and we've already reached our goal! People love you, Katy! Look everyone has donated. Linda and Anthony Wagner, Tommy Getter, Manny Estero, and even Hannah Glamour! Look at this! Kirov Koffee donated ten thousand dollars! This is incredible!"

Katy can't believe it! She hugs Izzy and says, "you are so amazing Izzy! I can't believe you did this!"

Izzy taps Katy's hand, "you'd do it for me!"

"Absolutely!" Katy agrees. "Now I wanna help you with Crusher Christine. She cheated in that match you guys had. She had a handful of tights that she used for leverage to get the pin!" Izzy's face drops and she tells Katy "Christine pulling my tights was my saving grace. She had me beat. I was wiped out. I had no strength left to try and kick out. When I felt her do that, I was relieved, she gave me a way to save face with the fans. Everyone saw her cheating. She gave me way too much credit that I still had some fight left in me. When the ref hit the count of three, she realized she didn't need to pull my tights. She could have had a clean win. She was thrilled to be the new champion but mad that she tainted her win for no reason."

Katy sits up straight and reassures Izzy, "You are the best I've ever seen. You will beat her! I'm going to watch as many of her matches as I can find on YouTube. I will find a weakness; I promise you that. I will even watch your match with her, and I guarantee I will find parts of that match where you had her beat."

Izzy runs around from behind the bar and gives Katy a huge hug.

A week has gone by and it seems that the case might have gone cold. When Special Agent Tim Horner of the FBI comes into Katy's office. He introduces himself, "we don't normally do this, but this case has extenuating circumstances. I'm getting pressure from the higher ups to close this mess before it makes the news."

Katy asks, "how can I help?"

Agent Horner says "you know this town and apparently the people here all love you. I was told that the only good police investigator is Detective Sanders, but I don't want to have to share any of the credit with LT Franklin. So, I'm here asking you. We've been monitoring every art dealer and auction house from here to Timbuktu and it's been complete radio silence. I have a feeling somebody here knows something but is unwilling to talk to the FBI. I feel you can be a great asset in solving this case."

Katy is flattered but simply replies "ok, I will try. But can you tell me what you think? Do you feel it's the Russian government doing this or just someone who is just in it for the money?"

"This whole thing screams Russian government." Agent Horner confesses to her. "...from the jammer used to scramble all the security cameras to the drugs that we found in the security guard's coffee. For one, they drugged the security guard just enough so that he would pass out for only a very short time. And then, there is the placement of the painting in the corner. It was left hidden from the view of the cameras. So, once the security guard came to and checked the cameras, he wouldn't notice a thing. He would've just thought that he had dozed off for a moment. This case screams Russian government involvement! Screams Russian Involvement too much. It's a school of red herrings. And that's why I don't think the case involves the Russian Government at all. I feel it's all about money."

"That's terrible!" Katy exclaims. "Someone would risk an international incident just to become rich. People are dying in the Ukraine. They trusted us to safeguard their precious artworks. Sir, I'm here to help and will do my best."

Agent Horner thanks Katy and leaves. Ray immediately comes in and declares, "ha! I knew it. They have nothing. They need my secret weapon Katy Rachford super investigator!"

Katy laughs, "I don't know about that, but you do know once I get involved with something I don't let it go!"

Katy swings by the welding shop where Eddie Galindo works. He sees her coming and cries "OMG! What do you want now? Is Ray going to kill me for talking to you?". There is actual fear in his voice.

Katy answers, "don't worry, I have carte blanche on this one. Have you heard anything about some stolen art?"

"I know who robbed who and who has the best drugs in town. But stolen art is not my forte. That's an extremely small group of people who deal in that. The only guy I know who might know anything about that is Frankie the Finger!"

Katy looks at Eddie a bit skeptically, "Frankie the Finger?! Why is he named that?"

Eddie tells her, "He used to be a snitch for the cops, and he would point out to the police the people who did the crime. That's until he got screwed over by former LT Toomey. He went to jail and the name stuck. But while inside he learned all about art. Weird, right? But I guess everyone has their thing."

"So how can I get in touch with this Mr. Finger?" Katy asks Eddie.

"He hangs out at the OTB. Besides art he really loves betting on the ponies." Eddie replies with a grin. "Tell him Eddie sent you. You had better stop at the ATM to have some cash ready. Oh yeah, I'd better see a carton of Newports at my shop by next week for this. I will waive my normal fee. Just get me the smokes."

Katy shouts "will do!" as she heads off to the OTB.

Katy shows up at the OTB and sees a man wearing an Andy Warhol tee shirt.

"Yup", she thinks, "that must be the guy." She walks up and says "hello, my name is Katy, Eddie said you might be able to help me."

Frankie looks her up and down and says, "bet on Darling Dandy to win in the third race."

Katy shakes her head, "no, no. I need some help with artwork."

Frankie is now really confused but asks, "what do you want to know?"

"Have you heard anything about an art heist?"

Frankie looks around before saying, "let's step outside."

They go behind the building and Frankie asks, "are you taking about the Ukrainian art that was lifted from the museum?"

"Yes!" Katy exclaims. "What do you know about it?"

"Not much, just that the Russian mob and the Feds are extremely interested in it. I did hear that some pasty-faced white dude might have planned the whole thing. He must know art but I don't think he is a real thief. He apparently pulled off the heist but, now, is running scared. He doesn't know what to do! He just has it hidden and is waiting for things to die down."

"Who is he? How do you know this?"

Frankie shrugs. "I hear things. I don't know him. I don't even know if any of that is true."

"Ok! Thank you. Keep me posted if you hear anything."

Frankie clears his throat. "Umm, a crisp Ben Franklin will go a long way right now."

Katy rolls her eyes and hands him the money.

Katy changes gears and goes to the lumberyard to use the ring for practice and training with Izzy. They know that to win, they have to really step up their game and train hard. Katy puts on her workout clothes and heads to the ring. There she sees Izzy with two other ladies.

Katy gets in the ring and Izzy tells her, "Jenny hired Yuki Hamada the Japanese assassin to train her." Izzy then turns to one of the ladies and introduces her to Katy, "This is Miko Tanaka Yuki's old partner. She feels what Jenny is doing is wrong and is here to teach you everything you need to know to counter Jenny's new strategy." After that, Izzy, gestures to the second woman, "This other fine lady is Dangerous Danica she came all the way from Canada to help me beat Christine. Danica helped train Christine before she became a jerk."

"Wow!" an impressed and grateful Katy tells them. "Thank you, ladies, so much."

"What do we do now?" Katy asks.

Izzy thinks for a second and then turns and looks at Katy, "you and Miko talk outside the ring and get to know each other. Make sure you pick her brain for anything useful while Danica and I have a training match. Then after us you two can go at it!"

Katy says "great idea Izzy. Good luck!" Katy and Miko exit the ring.

Danica and Izzy lock up. Danica overpowers Izzy and tosses her across the ring. She runs up and scoop slams Izzy to the mat! Bam! You can hear the impact echo throughout the gym. Izzy arches her back in pain as Danica begins to stomp the life out of her. Danica coos "come on Izzy! Christine is coming a long way to finish you off. She won't show you any mercy!" With that Izzy catches Danica's boot as she goes for another stomp. Izzy yanks Danica's foot and trips her to the mat. Izzy jumps up on fire. She yanks Danica off the mat and whips her into the ropes. Danica springs off and tries to hit Izzy with a high cross body block. Izzy ducks underneath and Danica crashes to the mat. Izzy leaps up and connects with a knee drop to Danica's forehead. Izzy has knocked her silly. Katy and Miko watch from outside of the ring in amazement! Izzy crashes down on Danica and goes for the pin. Izzy counts one when Danica throws her off. Izzy's face has a look of concern as Danica goes on the attack. She tells Izzy "Christine was a weightlifter. She is strong as hell. She is also tough as nails. She would hire two girls to fight her at once." She really lays into Izzy. She uses her size and strength advantage to make Izzy suffer. She continues to pummel and pound Izzy into the mat. Izzy narrowly avoids several near pins. She looks like she is finished, Danica yells at Izzy "get up! Fight back. This is the point in the match where Christine is the most vulnerable. She is over-confident. You need to dig deep and strike hard and fast. She has a weak jaw. You need to lure her in then connect with an elbow strike or grab her head and ram it into your knee. Then you need to trap her in a small package. She is too big and is unable to unfold herself quickly."

Izzy is on the mat wiped out. She says "I can barely move. How can I go on the offensive?" Danica screams, "this is how!" She begins to body slam Izzy to the mat repeatedly!

Katy yells "stop! You're going to kill her!"

Izzy mutters "no Katy, it's ok. I'm building resistance to the beating. Keep it up Danica. If I can survive this, then I can survive anything."

Danica tells Izzy, "See? You have the heart of a Champion. But that's enough for today. We will battle again tomorrow." Danica points at Katy and says "ok, get in here and show us what you got!"

Katy and Miko get in the ring. They circle around and attack. Miko quickly spins behind Katy grabs her by the waist and arches back!! Oh my! Miko dropped Katy right on the back of her head. Katy is seeing stars. Miko warns "Yuki strikes like a cobra. She will definitely teach that move to Jenny. Get up!" Katy staggers to her feet and goes to lock up with Miko. But Miko dives down and grabs Katy's ankles and Katy slams to the mat. Miko holds her feet and does a front flip. She arches her back and has Katy pinned. She counts "1! 2! Thr…!" When Katy barely kicks out. Miko cautions "you're lucky that Jenny won't be able to master these moves so quickly. But she will still be deadly. I need you to be stronger and faster than Jenny. She is out to hurt you. Katy you need to forget that she was your friend. She is now the enemy. Your job is to end the match as quickly as possible. The longer it goes the dirtier the tricks she will employ. I've seen you wrestle, you are great, but Yuki is deadly, and Jenny is possessed. Let's keep going. I'm going to make you suffer. I need you to feel this and hate it so much that you will never let Jenny do this to you." So, they have one of the most intense training matches ever. In the end, Miko is victorious, but she is amazed by Katy's resolve. She tells Katy "You are a worthy adversary. Jenny is in real trouble."

Katy rolls herself out of the ring and thanks Miko, saying "my God! I pray I never have to face you in a real match."

They hug and Katy goes to the shower.

Katy sits under the hot water and groans in pain.

Izzy yells from outside, "Let the water soak in. It helps."

After they showered and recovered a bit, they walk out to their cars and Katy rhetorically asks, "what the hell was that? That was probably the worst beating I've ever taken but it was probably the one of most valuable lessons that I have ever learned."

Izzy leans on Katy and dramatically accentuates "ouch!" by opening her mouth really wide.

"You're so right. Look out Jenny and Christine."

Another week has passed with no new leads in the case. But Katy and Izzy have really improved their skills thanks to Miko and Danica. Katy leans back in her desk chair when she gets a text from a strange number: "We are watching you. We will text you tonight about a location to meet up. Don't tell a soul, because if you do, we will know and the deal we have for you is off." Katy immediately dials the phone number but an automated message plays "the number you have reached is not in service."

Katy mutters "Crap! They used a spoofed phone number."

Ray walks in and asks, "did you say something?"

"Uh, no, just thinking out loud."

Ray tells Katy, "This happens sometimes, a case can move fast and furious and others can be super slow. Then, there are cases like this one that might never get solved. Hmm, I think I got a message on my machine from a lady who thinks her husband is cheating. Those are easy moneymakers."

Katy laughs, "yes, they are! But I'm not giving up quite yet."

Ray slaps Katy's desk and hollers, "that's my girl. Keep at it, tiger!"

Katy checks her phone and sees a text from Izzy: "did you hear about the warm up match that Jenny had? She put that rookie Zooming Zoe in the hospital. It was her debut event. I bet Zoe never tries to wrestle again. Jenny has become vicious, Katy. We need to be extra careful."

Katy texts back "OMG! That's awful. I guess I never really knew the real Jenny. This is such a shame. But thank you Izzy. You always have my back. XO XO!"

All the thoughts in Katy's head keep spinning around. She ponders how did someone pull off the art heist then completely vanish? Then she remembers all the good times that she had with Jenny. All the trials and tribulations that they went through. How they stuck together against all the adversity that the Air Force threw at them. She laughs, then she cries. But she regains her composure, "that's it. No more moping! I'm going to solve this case and then take care of the Jenny dilemma."

Katy is at home with Izzy cooking dinner when she gets a text: "be at the corner of Main Street and Water in an hour. Tell no one. You are being watched. Park around the corner on Lincoln."

Katy quickly finishes eating and goes to run out the door.

Izzy stops her. "Hey! Where are you going? What are you up to?"

"It's ok I just have to go out for a bit."

Izzy looks at her suspiciously, "hmm, I don't know. I don't have a good feeling about this. I'm going with you."

"No, no!" Katy pleads, "I must do this alone. But please use the track my phone app to monitor where I am."

Suspiciously, Izzy asks, "if nothing is wrong then why do I have to track you?"

Katy answers, "it's always better to safe than sorry."

Reluctantly, Izzy agrees and says, "I hate this but ok, now you better not leave town or I'm immediately calling the police."

"Thank you, Izzy. You really do always have my back."

And with that, Katy runs out the door.

Katy drives downtown. She parks on Lincoln as instructed. She walks to Main and Water where she sees a man tied up and gagged in the back of a pickup truck sitting next to the Portrait of Marshal Konev. She observes that the painting is in a brand-new gold frame and that the painting looks like it's been touched up a bit. She removes the gag.

The man, gasping for air, starts to spit out a confession. "I did it! I did it! I confess to everything. Look I wrote out my complete confession."

Katy doesn't believe a word. "No way! You're Mr. Vanderman! I can't believe you did this?" "Yes! I did it! I did. Please take me to jail.", he begs.

Katy leaves Mr. Vanderman tied up and calls Agent Horner.

"Hello Agent Horner, meet me at the corner of Main and Water I have a surprise for you."

A short time later, Agent Horner drives up like a manic. He screeches to a halt and jumps out of his car.

"What the hell? Did you do all this?", he yells at Katy.

"Nope just an anonymous tip." Katy beams.

He takes the painting and with relief says, "oh thank God it's safe. Holy crap, this case has been a nightmare! Nothing but constant harassment from DC."

Agent Horner calls the Cavalry, and six FBI officers show up.

"Hey, take the painting and Mr. Vanderman into custody." He tells them.

Agent Horner then turns to Katy, "great job Katy! But I'm going to need you to do a full debrief as soon as possible."

"Absolutely sir!"

Katy walks back to her car and is about to open the door when an SUV with very tinted windows pulls up beside her. The window rolls down and it's Viktor, Mr. Metroff's bodyguard.

"Get in.", he demands.

Katy gets into the back and sitting next to her is Dimitri Metroff.

"Hello Miss America, how are you?"

Katy snaps back with "you did this? How? Why? I want answers!"

Viktor slams on the brakes, turns around and in a very dry tone asks, "boss, do you want me to beat her?"

Dimitri gives a hearty laugh. "Oh, how I love the big set of balls on this one! No worries, Viktor."

Katy, not seeing the humor in the situation at all, asks "why did you do this? Was the 'Portrait of a Young Man' hiding behind Marshal Konev? If so, what did you do with it?"

Dimitri looks at Katy and states, "as I have told you before. I'm a noble businessman. I just wanted to have peace, I did it for the good of the world. Who needs more international incidents?"

Was that sincerity? Katy can't tell. She says "yeah ok, but what about the Raphael painting? Where is it?"

Dimitri answers. "All I can tell is that Vladimir is very happy that this painting was returned safely. He is also extremely happy about a new edition to his private collection. But I know nothing about where he got his new edition."

Katy yells at Dimitri, "you're full of crap! You took it!"

Viktor, now eyeing Katy through the rearview mirror, advises in a gruff voice, "watch your language with my boss."

Dimitri looks right into Katy's eyes. He holds her gaze, "everybody is happy now and you should be too. I heard you had a friend who betrayed you. I hate betrayal. If someone betrays me, they have an unfortunate accident. A very loud and gruesome accident. Not that I do such things. I just pray out loud and the people I pray about have accidents. Should Miss Jenny have an unfortunate accident?!"

The blood drains from Katy's face. She starts to babble, "Oh please no! She is just angry and bitter. So please again, no accidents. I will handle Jenny. But I did see a large donation to my Go Fund Me page from Kirov Koffee. Is that money clean? If it is clean, then I thank you. If it isn't, please, take it back."

"Kirov Koffee is very legitimate," Dimitri laughs. "We donate to lots of charitable causes. Nothing to worry about Miss America!" Then, he turns serious again, "Now if Jenny ever needs to have an accident you just say Stalin wears a nice hat when you order soup from Tatiana's. Now get out. I have business to attend to."

They drop Katy at her car and speed off.

Ray is waiting for Katy to come into work. When she does, he escorts her into his office.

"I know I gave you free reign in this one but.... Dimitri Metroff?! Katy! This isn't a game!" Ray scolds her.

Then Ray takes a deep breath and lets it out, "He seems nice but let me tell you, he also has a dark side. But as much as I am mad at you, I'm also extremely proud. You used your self-made connections to recover the painting."

Katy says "yes, but do you think Vanderman was solely responsible?"

"Me personally?" Ray says, "Of course not, but the FBI and the Museum are happy with it so that's good enough for us."

Katy interjects, "but I think Metroff stole the 'Portrait of a Young Man' painting. I'm sure if the FBI really puts the screws to Vanderman he will tell them what Metroff did."

"I can't guarantee much in this world, but I can absolutely guarantee that Vanderman will never mention anything about Metroff taking the Raphael piece."

"So, what's next?" Katy asks Ray.

Ray looks at Katy in bewilderment then says "what's next? You need to fix that problem with Jenny, give that your full undivided attention. We, umm, more like you did it. You got the stolen painting back. Everyone is happy. Well, everyone except Franklin, but he deserves to lose one. Now, get out of here. Go plan your next war move against the evil forces of Jenny Ryan."

Katy and Izzy are in the dressing room getting ready for a night that will definitely change their lives in one way or another. They go over last-minute strategies but mostly just sit and try to relax. When in walks a blast from the past! It's Tommy Getter. He runs up to Izzy and cries out, "boy, are you a sight for sore eyes. You look magnificent. But don't you worry about a thing Izzy, if you get beat up tonight, I'm just the guy to nurse you back to health. I'm in Med School!"

Izzy gives him a big hug, "oh how I missed your goofball machismo! Thank you. But I'm not planning on getting lumped up too bad."

Tommy then looks over at Katy, "whoa Katy! I don't like that look on your face. It looks like you're carrying the weight of the world on your shoulders. I think everyone in this place tonight is behind you one hundred percent. I know I am. I think I even saw Bobby and Becky Jasper out there."

Katy tells him, "I know Tommy, I need to let go. You're right. Thank you for coming all this way for us. We really appreciate it."

"That's my job ladies. I'm your knight in shining armor."

Izzy laughs and kicks Tommy out the door. As he leaves Betty Bass comes in. She puts both Katy and Izzy in a bear hug.

"I came all the way from Florida for this. I love you girls. I know you will make me proud. That Jenny needs a good butt kicking! Flatten her tonight, Katy!" Betty tells them.

Then from behind, Katy gets a tap on the shoulder. It's Pazia Ponderosa.

"Listen Katy," Pazia says, "I took three flights from Mexico to see you smack that B word down. You'd better do it, or I will. Man, she is trying to act like me now."

Everyone leaves and it's just Katy and Izzy. They hold hands until they call for Izzy. Katy gives her a final hug and says "you're the best Izzy! I mean the absolute best. Remember that. Take it to her!"

Izzy enters the ring to the roar of the crowd. She looks across and sees Christine pacing like a caged animal. Izzy doesn't even hear the ring announcer giving the introductions. She is laser focused on Christine. The bell rings and Christine charges at Izzy with murderous intent. But Izzy isn't backing down. She leaps up and nails Christine with a knee to the chest as she tries to level Izzy with a high cross body block. Both ladies crash to the mat, but it's Christine who took the hardest hit. She grabs her chest as Izzy pops up and gives it a stomp. The crowd cheers as she picks up Christine and flings her into the corner. Izzy follows up with a hand spring back elbow shot to the face! Christine collapses in the corner. Izzy grabs Christine behind her knees and monkey flips her across the ring. Christine lands with a thud! She holds her stomach and rolls around on the mat! Izzy is pumped and lets out a scream! But as Izzy reaches down to pick up Christine, she gets her face raked by Christine's nails. Izzy staggers back while Christine jumps up in a rage. She unloads on Izzy with a vicious assault! The match becomes an all-offensive affair by Christine. She ruthlessly repeatedly body slams Izzy to the mat! Tommy can barely look! Then Christine hits Izzy with a power bomb! The crowd gasps as Izzy isn't moving. Christine parades around the ring flipping off the crowd as they shower her with boos! She leaps up and slams down on Izzy!

She yells "this is it!" As the ref counts 1! 2...thr...! No way! Izzy stays alive! She got her shoulder only a millimeter off the mat, but that was just enough! Christine pushes her shoulder back down and screams at the ref to count again! So, he slaps the mat for the 1! 2!..and a kick out!! Christine pops up and screams at the ref! Izzy rolls around on the mat and gets to her knees as Christine turns around! Izzy hits her with a shot to the gut! Then another! Izzy gets up shaking her fists and stomping her feet! The crowd goes crazy! Izzy and Christine are toe to toe trading blows! Izzy swoops down and picks up Christine in a fireman's carry! Then with an incredible feat of strength tosses Christine over her head and slams Christine's mid-section across her knee! Christine lets a scream! Izzy jumps on Christine's back and applies a Cobra Clutch!! Wow are we back in the WWF in 1983?! Sgt Slaughter would be proud. Izzy has her in the center of the ring! Izzy squeezes with all her might as Christine, showing tremendous strength, gets to her feet! It looks like she is going to make it to the ropes and break the hold. But as she is only inches away, she collapses back to the mat! She is out! The referee raises her arm once, twice, and three times it falls! The ref tells Izzy to release the hold! It's over! It's all over! Izzy falls to the mat exhausted! So, the ref picks her up and over the speakers, the ring announcer declares, "the winner of this heart pounding match is Isabelle the lady warrior Salinas!!" The crowd jumps up and down in sheer joy!

Back in the dressing room Izzy can barely stand.

Katy congratulates Izzy, "Izzy! You did it! That was the most amazing thing I've ever seen! I'm in awe!"

Izzy takes Katy's hand. "I don't know how I survived. I felt like quitting! I guess the beating that Danica gave me actually was a blessing. It saved me in this match!". She then struggles to her feet and looks Katy straight in the eye. "Now I want you to go teach Jenny a lesson. She just can't betray her friends. Now she is going to use your love of her against you! Don't let her. So for the next few minutes she is just an evil opponent out to destroy you! Take her out before she takes you out!"

Katy gives Izzy a hug, "You're my rock Izzy! I will make you proud! I will repay her for how she betrayed us!"

Katy gets a tap on the shoulder and is told to head to the ring! The second she appears through the back curtain the crowd goes absolutely wild!!! Katy high fives and hugs the fans all the to the ring. She hops into the ring and sees Jenny staring at her from the opposite corner. Jenny has a look of both fear and anger. Katy stares back with complete disappointment in her eyes. Katy yells over to her "why Jenny? Why?"

Then the ring announcer gets on the microphone, "Ladies and gentlemen, this is our main event of the evening! It's a special grudge match! Two former best friends and tag team partners who are now bitter foes! Hanging in the balance of the outcome of the match is the knowledge of who the superior athlete is! Also hanging in the balance is the fate of a one of kind piece of literary fiction! This will be a match people will be talking about for many years to come! Introducing, first, in the corner to my right is Jenny Moneybags Ryan!"

The crowd unleashes a torrent of boos and hisses at Jenny! She just stands there fixated on Katy!

Then the ring announcer says, "and in the corner to my left…everyone's favorite sweetheart, the one, the only, Gorgeous Katy!!!!!"

The crowd explodes with cheers as they chant "we love you, Katy!"

The bell sounds and the two ladies engage in a tactical chess match! They poke and prod at each other looking for an opportunity to strike! Then Jenny lunges at Katy trying to get behind her and apply the German Suplex move that Yuki taught her. But Katy sees it coming and leaps over the top of a bent over Jenny! Katy catches her around the waist and wraps her up in a sunset flip! The ref counts 1! 2! Thre! When Jenny barely kicks out! Wow! This match was almost over that quickly! Jenny rolls out of the ring to rethink her strategy! The crowd calls her a coward as she paces around the outside of the ring. The ref starts to count Jenny out when Katy sits on the second rope, making an opening for Jenny to return to the ring.

"Come Jenny, let's finish this feud right now!" Katy sneers.

Jenny is stunned by Katy's gesture and climbs back in! The two ladies circle and lock up. The match becomes pretty even but everyone can sense that Katy is holding something back. She doesn't seem to capitalize when the opportunity presents itself. She lets Jenny escape defeat more than once. Then after being whipped into the corner, Jenny pulls what appears to be a capsule from inside the top of her outfit. She bites down on it and sprays a green mist into Katy's eyes! That's definitely an old Japanese pro wrestling trick that she must have learned from Yuki! Katy is completely blinded by the mist and staggers back against the ropes. The ref admonishes Jenny as she assaults Katy with a blistering barrage of punches and knee strikes! The crowd boos intensely! Jenny takes a blinded and battered Katy and snaps her to the mat! Katy desperately tries to wipe the mist out of her eyes while Jenny yanks Katy's hair and she violently shakes her head back and forth! Katy is on the mat in serious trouble.

Jenny yells at the crowd "this is who you love? I'm going to torture her and make her scream!"

The crowd is in shock as Jenny picks up Katy and slaps her across the face! Wow! How insulting! She then whips Katy into the ropes. Katy springs off and Jenny grabs Katy's hair and drives her face first into the mat! That's it folks! The crowd can barely watch as Jenny covers Katy for the pin! Jenny hooks Katy's tights for extra leverage as the ref counts 1! 2!!!! OMG!!! That was 2 and nine tenths! That was probably the narrowest escape in wrestling history!! Jenny gets up in utter disbelief! She shoves the referee to the mat and runs over to the corner turnbuckle! Does everyone see this? Jenny is pure evil! She removes the padding from the corner exposing the bare metal!

Jenny picks up Katy and yells to the crowd "I'm going to bust her wide open! Say goodbye to Gorgeous Katy!" Jenny proceeds to whip Katy face first into the metal when Holy Cow! Katy puts on the brakes and reverses the move!

Jenny goes flying in, face first! Wow! Jenny staggers back with a huge gash on her forehead! Katy spins Jenny around and hits her with boot to the midsection! Jenny doubles over in pain! Stone Cold Stunner!!! Stone Cold Stunner!! Gorgeous Katy hits Jenny with a Stone-Cold Stunner! Jenny got rocked! The crowd explodes as Katy pounces on Jenny as the ref counts 1! 2!!………3!!!!!!! It's deafening here inside the arena! I've never seen a crowd yell so loud! Katy manages to get to her feet with her bloodshot eyes and that green mist still on her face!

The referee raises her hand as the ring announcer can't hold back his elation, "unbelievable! Incredible! The winner of the match....... Gorgeous Katy!!"

This place is on fire with excitement! But Jenny just rolls out of the ring and slinks away.

The crowd chants "we want the book! We want the book!"

But Jenny is gone!

Katy somehow manages to stumble back to the dressing room where Izzy is waiting with a warm washcloth and eye drops! Katy sits in a chair while Izzy cleans her up.

Katy asks, not really expecting an answer, "Who was that monster in the ring? How could that have been Jenny?! She was pure evil!"

"Something must have snapped in her head. To make matters worse she told Christine Caruso to burn your book if she lost! Christine might be a villain in the ring, but she is no monster!" Izzy replies.

Izzy then hands Katy her Agatha Christie book.

Katy holds it tightly, "please thank Christine for me! This was a gift from my deceased Grandmother!"

"I already did!" Izzy says.

Suddenly, Tommy Getter, Betty Bass, Ray Enzo, Tamara Sanders and Pazia Ponderosa burst into the room! They are all a buzz talking about the match when Pazia says "does Jenny want to wrestle full time in Mexico? They love evil women down there!"

They all laugh.

Betty comments, "I don't know about Mexico, but I know of another place that's really hot where she can go!"

Ray finally speaks up, "ok! Everybody out! Katy needs some alone time!"

As they all leave Ray walks back in and says "rest up my dear, I have a buddy who might need help with a special case. I want you to just provide some psychological analyses of some of the possible suspects and nothing else!"

Katy does her famous fourth wall break and smiles as she says "absolutely Ray! Nothing else!"

Blur's "Song 2" begins to play!!